ALL THE RIGHT MOVES

MICHELLE HERCULES

Cover Design: Michelle Hercules
Photographer: Eric Battershell
Models: Tessi Conquest & Jamie Walker

Editor: Hot Tree Editing

Paperback ISBN: 978-1-950991-33-4

PROLOGUE
EMMA

January 2016, California

Do you know that cliché scene of a drunken chick, sticking out of a limousine's sunroof top and yelling nonsense to the wind? That's me, wearing a stupid-ass plastic crown and holding a bottle of champagne. Classy. I can check that off my to-do list—not that I have a list of ridiculous things to accomplish before I die, but if I did, that would've been ticked off using a thick Sharpie. I not only did it, I nailed it. Shit, I would've flashed a family in a minivan if Peyton, the bride-to-be, hadn't pulled me back down into the car.

"You're crazy. You're gonna get us arrested," she says between giggles.

"Oh, if it's a sexy cop, I'm down for that." I laugh.

Funny how twenty minutes ago, I was regretting my decision to not hop onto a flight to Brussels soon after New Year's Eve like I'd planned. I let Peyton, one of my friends from high school, guilt me into postponing my trip so I could join her bachelorette party. We were close during our teen years—she was the daughter of a movie mogul, and my father was the top celebrity lawyer in Hollywood. We were considered royalty in school. However, what really made us bond were our views about the opposite sex. Guys were toys, and we got bored of them easily.

Once we graduated high school, we slowly drifted apart. She went to study in Switzerland and I stayed here in California. We kept in touch—meaning, I followed her Instagram account—but I can no longer call her my bestie like I used to. When she told me she was getting married, I thought she was joking. She was worse than me when it came to objectifying boys. But here we are, celebrating her last days as a single woman in the only way she knows how, with loads of alcohol, drugs, and debauchery.

The longer the evening progresses, the louder our group becomes. Besides Peyton, I only know two other girls: her older sister Vicky, and Samara, Peyton's roommate in Switzerland whom I met years ago when I went to visit. But several bottles of champagne later, I'm as thick as thieves with the entire group.

We're ten in total, crammed together in the biggest limo one can rent, going to an unknown destination. It's loud inside the moving vehicle, with Lady Gaga's "Alejandro" blasting through the speakers and the cacophony of voices singing together completely off-key.

Vicky stands on shaky legs, then falls on her ass after a couple of steps. We holler and whistle, and she flips us all off.

"Shut up, bitches." Bracing on her hands, she gives up on standing and kneels in the middle of the floor instead.

"It's time for a little surprise, y'all. I've got some molly!" She waves a clear plastic bag with small white pills inside.

"Fuck yeah!" Peyton raises the glass of champagne in her hands.

Vicky begins to distribute the drug of choice if you're rich and famous, but when she offers me the bag, I shake my head. "No, no. I'm good."

"That's fucking bull crap, Emma. Take it." Peyton glares at me from across the limo.

As if you on cue, everyone begins to chant, "Take it, take it, take it."

"Ah fuck. Why the hell not." I pull a pill from the bag and swallow it with the help of champagne. Sure, I caved to peer pressure, but this is probably my last wild night for a long time. Might as well go out with a bang.

"Where are we going now?" one of Peyton's friends asks.

The limo comes to a stop and Vicky announces we've arrived. One by one, we get out of the car, but as hard as everyone is trying, not a single one of us can make a dignified exit. I'm lucky I don't trip and fall on my face. The cold winter air hits my naked arms, and I realize I forgot my jacket in the limo. I try to go back for it, but someone—Peyton, it seems—pulls my arm and drags me to a busy promenade that looks oddly familiar. It's not until I catch a whiff of the ocean scent that my brain makes the connection. We're in Hermosa Beach.

"What's the plan?" I ask to no one in particular.

"It's a pub crawl," Vicky yells from the front of the group.

Whistles follow us, but that's because we're making a ruckus as we go. I soon forget the cold, distracted as I am by the euphoric feeling pumping in my veins. Vicky picks the first bar, an Irish pub by the looks of the décor—classic dark wood furniture, brown leather booths, several different kinds of beer on tap. It's busy and we'll be hard-pressed to find a table. That's not the plan, though. Instead, Vicky carves up space for herself at the bar and orders shots for us.

While I wait, I glance at the place, checking out the male assortment. Would it be bad if I hooked up with someone tonight? I'm feeling kind of needy.

I sigh loudly, not seeing anyone interesting, until I turn and watch a sex god walk out of the kitchen carrying a tray of food. Holy fuck! I think I might just orgasm from staring at him. He's the most gorgeous man I've ever seen. Okay, maybe that's the booze and molly talking, but he does give Chris Hemsworth a run for his money. Just as tall as the actor—I've met Chris in person—and built like a fortress, that sexy waiter is exactly what I need tonight.

"Earth to Emma." Peyton shakes my arm. "Here's your shot."

I reluctantly peel my gaze from my target and take the offered glass. It's tequila. Jesus, the hangover tomorrow will be a bitch, but if everything goes according to plan, I'll be getting over that while riding Mr. Delicious.

I already have a nice buzz going on, and the tequila goes straight to my head.

Peyton whistles appreciatively next to me, and I know she's spotted my guy. Her behavior makes all the girls turn to gawk at him, and before anyone can say anything, I yell, "Dibs! I call dibs."

"Shut up. You can't call dibs on that!" Vicky says.

"I can and I did."

Peyton crosses her arms and levels me with a glare. "You're not going to ditch us to chase some hot piece of ass. I forbid it."

"Will you relax? I'm not ditching you, but excuse me while I go lay down the groundwork for later."

I fix my dress, making sure my cleavage is on full display, then I veer toward the back of the pub. Mr. Delicious is serving a table at the moment, but I know he'll eventually get back to the kitchen, so I wait for him near the door. Not a minute later, he comes striding toward me and I make my move, blocking his way.

"Hi," I say.

"Uh, hi? Can I help you?"

"I sure hope you can." I smile coyly. "We're celebrating my

best friend's bachelorette party, and I've been tasked with raising money for drinks."

"Okay?" Mr. Delicious narrows his eyes a bit and he's not smiling, but at least he didn't tell me to get lost yet. *Shit, he won't be an easy one to snatch. I need to bring my A game.*

I shove my hand inside my purse and pull out a string of condoms we all got as party favors. They're wrapped in pink foil and have Peyton's picture on them. "Would you be interested in buying some?"

He raises both eyebrows as he stares at the ridiculous condoms.

"So, help a girl out?" I bat my eyelashes, exaggerating the gesture on purpose.

"I'm sorry," he says, still eyeing the party favors dangling from my fingers. "I'm rather busy, and I don't have any cash on me right now."

Fuck a duck. I wasn't expecting that answer. But my disappointment only lasts a split second, because he just gave me the perfect opening to seal the deal.

"That's okay. I'll come back for the money later." I shove the condoms in his hand and walk away before he can return them. Only when I'm at safe distance do I peer over my shoulder. Mr. Delicious is in the same spot I left him, condoms in hand and a stunned look on his face. Excellent.

Well played, Emma. Well played.

When I return to my friends, they're ready to go to the next bar. Peyton notices the Cheshire cat smile on my face and asks, "What did you do?"

"Oh nothing. Just made sure I have a reason to come back."

Rori

What the hell just happened here?

"Hey, boss. What do you have there?" Xavier, my bartender, asks.

"Condoms. Apparently I just bought some on credit." I walk around the bar, but now I can't remember what the hell my customer ordered.

"Oh yeah? From one of the bachelorette party's chicks? They were nuts, high as kites, but they just gave me a two-hundred-dollar tip on a hundred-dollar bill, so I'm not complaining."

"Come again?" I stop in my tracks.

Xavier raises both hands and steps back. "Don't give me that look. I didn't take advantage of them. I actually asked several times if they were sure. By the bling I spotted on some of them, I could tell they were rich. This was probably coupon money for them."

Strangely, that information doesn't sit well with me. I won't begrudge members of my crew a healthy tip, though; they all work hard, and they deserve it. I put the condoms away, shoving them in one of the shelves under the bar counter, and try to get that girl out of my mind. She was attractive, no doubt about that, but I've never had a good experience with rich chicks in the past. I have a problem being treated like property, or worse, like I'm a dumb jock. After a few bad apples, I tend to avoid having anything to do with them.

A minute later, Condom Girl is all forgotten. The pub is as busy as ever, and I don't have a minute to breathe, much less to think about a woman I'll never see again.

Around one in the morning, most of our patrons have gone home, and I give the signal to Xavier to announce closing time. As tradition, he puts on the song by Semisonic, and the regulars groan loudly, knowing it's the last round. The kitchen closed a couple hours ago, so I help Xavier on cleanup duty behind the bar. I'm crouching, hidden from view as I organize some bottles, when I hear Condom Girl's voice asking for me. How the fuck do I still remember what she sounds like? I spoke to her for less than a minute.

Shit. I really thought she wasn't going to come back.

"Uh, boss? I think someone is waiting for payment," Xavier chuckles.

I unfurl from my crouch and find Condom Girl standing on the other side, leaning against the chair as if she needs the support to remain upright. Her makeup is a little smeared, and her eyes are bloodshot.

Jesus. I can't believe she's still standing.

"Hi there. I came back." She gives me a lopsided smile. It would've been cute if she weren't drunk as a skunk.

I look in the door's direction. "Where are your friends?"

She shrugs. "Don't know. I ditched them to come back here before you closed."

I groan in my head. *Just fucking great. Now I have to deal with this.* I walk around the bar and when I'm almost in front of her, she turns, letting go of the chair. She stumbles over nothing and ends up falling into my arms. I don't know if she did it or purpose or not, but if she's trying to seduce me, she's wasting her time.

"Okay, lass. It's time to get you into a cab."

"My name is not lass. I'm Emma. And you are?" She looks at me from under her ridiculously long eyelashes, not the fake kind. Damn it. I shouldn't be noticing these things.

"Someone who's been on his feet all day and wants to go bed."

"Alone?" Hope shines in her big green eyes. I bet they're lovely when they aren't bloodshot.

"Yes. *Alone.*"

She steps away from my arms, frowning, then pulls a chair out to sit down. "Fine. Then go get my money."

Is she for real?

Shaking my head, I ask Xavier to hand me a twenty from the cash register. "All right, how much for the condoms?"

She plucks the bill from my fingers. "This will do."

"That's four dollars a pop," I say.

"Those are special condoms." She shoves the money down her cleavage and jumps off the chair with the grace of a giraffe on stilts. She can't walk a straight line as she heads for the door.

"Hmm, boss? You can't let her leave like that," Xavier says. "I'd offer to take her home, but I don't want to get in trouble with my lady."

"I know," I grunt. "Close everything, just don't put the alarm on." I pull my apron off and go after Emma, who's already disappeared through the door.

The promenade is much quieter now that all the restaurants are closed. Emma didn't make a lot of progress, and I find her curled forward with her hands braced on her knees. *Ah fuck. She's not puking, is she?*

"Are you okay?" I stop next to her, shoving my hands in my jeans pockets.

"No," she whimpers, not moving from her position.

"Do you need to throw up?"

She straightens up and takes a deep breath. "I don't think so. I'm light-headed and everything's fuzzy."

"What did you take?"

"Molly," she says without hesitation while she keeps staring ahead.

Of course. The drug of choice of rich fools.

I place a hand on her lower back and nudge her forward. "Come on. Let's get you home."

"I can't remember my address." Her voice raises to a shrill

pitch. "Oh my God. I think Peyton slipped me another pill before I left them."

Are these people nuts? Emma grips her hair, pulling at it like she's about to lose her shit.

"It's on your driver's license," I reply. When she doesn't respond, I add, "Your address. It's on your driver's license."

Still no response from her. I don't know what stage of her trip she's in. And worse, I have no idea how much alcohol she has in her system either. I'm debating whether I should just take her to the emergency room.

She finally looks at me with eyes a little clearer, but not by much. "Thank you for taking me home."

"Don't mention it," I say, a little grumpier than I intended.

She takes a step forward, still with difficulty, so to speed up our progression, I lace my arm with hers and pretty much drag her along. She takes advantage of the situation and nudges closer, resting her head against my arm. We get to the main street, and as fate would have it, there are no cabs in sight. I can't call an Uber—sometimes those drivers can be such creeps. Resigned, I head for my car parked two streets up.

Halfway there, Emma begins to rub my arm. "Thanks for thanking me home."

"You already said that." I should make her stop caressing me, but what would be the point? She's beyond getting a clue.

"I'll make it worth your while."

My nostrils flare as anger simmers in my gut. She's lucky I'm the one taking her home and not some perv who would take advantage of her in this state. I'm pissed her friends let her walk alone in this vulnerable condition, but they probably weren't thinking straight either.

I help Emma into my car, and by the time I walk around it and sit behind the steering wheel, her head's propped against the window and her eyes are almost closed. I don't move, paying attention to her breathing. It sounds normal.

I shake her arm lightly. "Emma?"

She blinks slowly, her eyes languid and sleepy. "Yes, Mr. Delicious?"

Mr. Delicious? Ah hell, I must've pissed some deity off.

"How are you feeling?"

Licking her lips, her gaze drops to my crotch. "Horny as fuck, if you must know. I can't wait to get you into my bed."

I grind my teeth because my cock is beginning to get onboard with that idea, even though my brain is screaming, *Abort, abort.*

"Do you always proposition men you don't know?"

"Not always. Only if they look and sound like you."

"Sound like me? I don't even know what that means."

"You sound like sex on a stick. I bet you could make me come just by whispering naughty things in my ear in that yummy accent of yours."

Damn it. My cock is totally awake now. I shouldn't have asked anything. I'm not a perv, and I've never slept with an intoxicated girl before or felt remotely inclined to do so. So why the hell do I have a boner now? I should be repulsed by Emma's attitude, not aroused by it.

"Driver's license, please," I say through clenched teeth.

"Eager, aren't you?" She giggles, thinking her seduction game is working on me.

She's not completely wrong, I think perversely. This is a sign that I need to get laid pronto if my dick is reacting to a chick who can barely walk straight.

She hands me her ID, and I recognize the address. "You go to DuBose College?"

"Yup. This is my final semester, but I'll be in Brussels on an internship until summer. Tonight is my final hoorah before I enter serious adulting territory, so I'm making it count."

By drinking like a fish, getting high, and picking up a stranger for a booty call. Jesus Christ. This kind of irresponsible stupidity hurts. Even when I was a teen, I didn't pull shit like that. Then again, I was focused. I knew exactly what I wanted, and nothing was getting in my way.

And look what happened in the end, the devil on my shoulder whispers in my ear.

My anger drops down a notch, turning into annoyance. I clamp my mouth shut and don't offer any more comments. Why waste my breath lecturing someone who clearly doesn't think she's doing anything wrong?

Without asking, Emma reaches for the radio, tuning it to an obnoxious pop music station. I guess it's better than her spending the fifteen-minute drive coming on to me.

When I pull over in front of her building, I'm half tempted to let her go in by herself, but my responsible side won't let me do that. I get out of the car and escort her to her floor. The elevator is out of service—of course it is—so we go up the three flights of stairs. The trip takes twice as long, thanks to Emma's lack of coordination. It would be faster if I just threw her over my shoulder and dragged her ass up.

She stops in front of a generic white door and announces it's her place. It takes forever for her to dig the key from her purse, and another minute for her to fit the damn thing in the hole. In a fit of giggles, she finally pushes the door open and kicks her shoes off. From the hallway, I see it's a nice apartment, big for college standards. She must have roommates.

Emma turns to me with a frown when I don't follow her in. "Aren't you coming?"

"Nope. Make sure you drink enough water before you go to bed."

Why am I giving her advice like I care? It'll serve her right to wake up with a massive hangover.

"I'd rather drink something else besides water." She reaches for my hand and drags me in. My feet take two steps forward before I make an effort to stop.

"Emma, please. Just go to bed. Trust me, you'll regret this tomorrow."

She leans closer, bringing her body flush against mine while pressing her hand against my chest. And goddamn she feels nice attached to me like that, despite her drunkenness and all.

"Don't worry, Mr. Delicious. I know exactly what I'm doing. I want you, and I always get what I want."

Bam! A bucket of cold water is dumped over my head. Her arrogance is exactly what I need to snap me out of this moment of insanity.

I pull her hand off my chest and take a step back.

"The name is Rori O'Shea. Not Mr. Delicious."

"Fine, *Rori O'Shea*. Now stop playing hard to get. I know you want me." She runs her hand over her body, like she's a cheap hooker showing off her goodies to entice clients. It's ridiculous and embarrassing.

I should give her a break—she's high on molly, after all, a drug known to lower one's inhibitions and increase libido—but I'm pissed at myself for not leaving already, and at her for being stupid.

"I'm heading off. Have a good night." I swing around and veer for the door.

"Wait. Are you leaving for real?" Genuine surprise laces her tone.

"Yes," I say over my shoulder.

Incredulity flashes in her eyes for a brief moment before her gaze turns into a glare.

"Fine. Suit yourself, Rori O'Shea. But I want you to leave with the knowledge that the only reason you're able to stand your ground, the only reason you're not in my bed yet, is because I don't want you. If I did, you would be on your knees, begging."

"Funny. Didn't you say a minute ago that you wanted me, and you always get what you want?"

"I lied."

She pushes me the final steps through the door and closes it in my face with a loud bang. Exactly the same reaction you would expect from a toddler who was denied a toy. She threw a fucking tantrum because I said no. My earlier assessment was right: entitled rich girl. If I never see her again, it'll be too soon.

So why the hell am I still planted here, staring at her fucking door?

1
———

EMMA

March 2016, Brussels

TODAY'S THE DAY. I'VE DECIDED IT. AFTER A MONTH OF obsessing about Mr. Hot Commuter, I'm going to talk to him—that is, if he shows up. I haven't seen him in two weeks, and I'm beginning to worry he's changed jobs, or worse, left the country. It happens a lot here in Brussels. People come for temporary jobs and then bye-bye.

I'm wearing the sexiest work appropriate outfit I own, a sharp jacket and pencil skirt by the late Alexander McQueen that fits me perfectly. I even curled my hair.

When the train approaches, I try a superhero move and scan the cars. A truly impossible task when the train is so busy. I'll just pick the car I always do, the one in the middle. I'm pretty much pushed inside when the door opens, and to avoid falling on my face, I go with the flow while craning my neck to see over the crowd.

I spot his mop of impeccable dark hair right away. He's standing toward the front with his head down, looking at his phone. Crap. I'm in the complete opposite end.

When the door closes and people have settled in their spots, I begin to make my way to him, hoping he doesn't look up while I'm elbowing my way through. I don't want to look desperate—which I totally am. Who knew it would be so hard to find man candy in this town?

Mr. Hot Commuter doesn't glance up from his phone, not even when people jolt him to get to the door. *Gee, what are you reading there, buddy?*

The train stops suddenly, throwing me against him since I didn't bother holding on to anything. Yeah, I was totally banking on that. A girl's gotta do what a girl's gotta do.

"Oops, sorry." I smile at him.

He's frowning at first, but then his expression changes when he sees my face. Guys are so predictable. His hand finds my arm and he helps steady me.

"Are you okay?"

"Yup. Trains are dangerous in high heels."

Mr. Hot Commuter glances down at my feet, and then his eyes slowly travel back up the length of my body. Things are unfolding exactly how I want them to. I still have game.

"You look familiar," he says, and I detect an accent, probably Irish.

"I do? I take this train every day."

"Yes, I know." He smirks at me. We've exchanged glances before and he remembers.

"So, you've noticed me."

"It's hard not to."

I raise an eyebrow, and his cheeks turn slightly red. "Where are you from?" I ask.

"Ireland. I couldn't hide the accent, could I?"

"Why hide?"

"Well, it's a little thick. Sometimes people have a hard time understanding me."

"I think it's lovely. Where in Ireland? I've only been to Dublin and Cliff de Moher."

"Kinsale. It's a small town."

"I bet it's nice."

My station is announced, so I'd better get things moving. "My name is Emma, by the way. And you are?"

"Declan Kelly. I work a—"

A deafening boom rattles my bones, and then my body is airborne. I don't see where I land, but sharp pain shoots up the side of my torso as white-hot agony takes over all my other senses. I try to scream and choke immediately on the smoke that surrounds me. The acrid smell in the air is suffocating. My ears are ringing, I can't draw air into my lungs, and panic sets in. In the distance, I hear screams, names being called. The sound is muffled, and as hard as I try, I can't make out words, can't figure out what's going on. The pain is too much. It's all I can feel.

Come on, Emma. Stand up.

I send the command to my muscles, but they don't register my will. I let out a whimper, closing my eyes. This is hopeless. All I can focus on is the pain and the fact that I can't move.

I'm not sure how long I lie there, almost half-dead, when someone touches my back and asks if I'm okay. A moan is the only answer I can manage. Then they try to lift me, but my body still won't cooperate. It's boneless.

"Can you walk?" a man asks.

"I don't know," I croak, and it feels like my throat's on fire. "What's going on?"

"I think there was a bomb. Come on. We need to get out of here."

He picks me up, which only makes my wound hurt ten thousand times more. I scream because no matter how hard I clench my jaw, there's no keeping that bottled inside.

"Shit, shit, shit," the man says. "Stay with me, Emma. We're getting out of here."

How does he know my name? I open my eyes, even though the smoke stings them, and focus on his face. I can only make out a squared jaw and the dimple on it, but it's enough for me to recognize my savior—Declan.

We start to move slowly, but once we're out of the mangled car, things don't improve. Gray smoke is everywhere, and it's so damn dark I begin to doubt we'll ever see the light of day again. The ringing in my ears subsides, replaced by a cacophony of panicked voices and cries. Over the noise, I'm able to hear someone shouting orders. Declan jumps off something, and my guess is that we're on the tracks now. I feel my strength waning, and I keep losing track of time as the world fades intermittently, like a lamp that's about to die.

I think I'm about to pass out completely when fresher air reaches my nose. We're out of the tunnel. The bright light is almost an assault to my senses.

"Help. I need help!" Declan shouts.

I blink and focus on his face. "Are you okay?"

"I'm fine, Emma. Stay with me okay? Help is on the way."

"You saved me."

"Of course I did. I wouldn't leave you behind."

He's covered in soot, and his forehead is bleeding. I try to remain awake, but it seems my body's had enough.

Help finds us, and suddenly I'm no longer in his arms. I want to tell him to not leave me, but it's too late. Everything fades to black, and he's gone.

2

———

EMMA

February 2017, New York

"I HAVE A CONFESSION TO MAKE." SCOTT FITZGERALD THE THIRD takes a sip of the five-hundred-dollar bottle of wine he insisted on ordering as he watches me over the rim of the glass.

"Oh?" I try to put some enthusiasm in my tone, but this date is going worse by the minute.

"I usually don't go on blind dates."

"Yeah, me neither." *And the reason being I get stuck with douchecanoes like yourself.* If I were in California, I would've set up a rescue system with one of my friends. Here, the only person I could attempt that is the very person who insisted I go out with Scott.

The man leans back in his chair with a smug smile on his face. "You get it, right? We're made out of the same cloth, Emma. We're both attractive and wealthy. Why should we waste our times with people beneath us? I'm glad Femke wasn't wrong about you."

My jaw slackens for a brief second before I recover and force my face into neutrality. I'm one second away from telling him exactly what I think about his asinine comment when I recognize the busboy. Ricky is a student at Columbia where I'm presently acquiring my MBA. He's the carbon copy of a younger Antonio Banderas, and more than ever, he's a sight for sore eyes. I met him while I was working on an assignment at the school's library, and we clicked immediately. We've flirted a little, but our schedules never allowed for more.

He turns and our gazes collide. A thousand-watt smile breaks on his face, right before he makes a beeline for our table.

"Hi, Emma. Long time no see."

"Hey, Ricky. It's been ages. How's school?"

Scott clears his throat, and the easygoing smile vanishes from Ricky's face. "Oh, I'm sorry. Am I interrupting your date?"

Scott says "Yes" at the same time I answer "No." Then he glares at me.

"Ricky is a friend from Colombia."

"Oh, I didn't know you were friends with the workers there," Scott says, making me curl my hands around my fork. *What an insufferable ass.*

"I don't work there. I *go* there," Ricky says in the most polite manner possible, but the clench of his jaw tells me he wants to punch my date.

"Well, you work here, right? Then do your job and clear our table. It's been minutes since we finished our starters, and our plates are still here. This is unacceptable."

A hint of anger shines in Ricky's eyes, and I feel awful and embarrassed that I'm having dinner with such an ass.

"Right away, sir," Ricky says without making eye contact with me.

He collects our plates and walks away. When he's out of earshot, I lean forward, my eyes nothing more than slits. "That was rude and unnecessary."

"No, he was rude. He had no business coming here to chat with you. Employees shouldn't socialize with patrons."

"I told you he's my friend."

Boldly, Scott covers my hand with his. "Oh, Emma. It's sweet that you want to include all classes in your circle, but it's not very practical. People like that guy are leeches who only want to take advantage of you."

I pull my hand from under Scott's and push my chair back with a loud screech. Throwing my napkin on the table, I stand up.

Scott's beady eyes turn as round as saucers. "Where are you going?"

"Isn't it clear, darling? I'm leaving."

"Are you serious?" His eyebrows shoot up to the heavens.

"Oh, I'm serious. It turns out Femke was dead wrong about you."

Flaring his nostrils, Scott shoots daggers at me with his eyes. Then he smiles without humor and shakes his head. "I should've known. What else could I expect from a born-and-raised Hollywood airhead?"

The insult puts a chink in my armor. I've lost count of the number of times people have called me by a derogative name—airhead, bimbo—just because I like to party and sleep around. No one seems to care that I graduated top in my class, or that I secured an internship in a top equity firm in New York City by my own merit. But I'll be damned if I let Scott see that he affected me with his words.

"Airhead? Wow, besides being an arrogant ass, you're also unoriginal. No surprise there. And by the way, your toupee is crooked."

I watch the blood drain from his face as he tries to fix his hair. I wouldn't have guessed he was wearing fake hair if I hadn't caught him messing with his toupee when he thought I wasn't looking.

Feeling victorious, I sashay toward the exit, ignoring the stares thrown my way. This crowd isn't used to dramatic scenes, it appears.

Outside, I'm about to ask the valet to flag me a cab when I catch Ricky coming out of the alley next to the restaurant.

"Ricky!" I wave at him.

He glances over his shoulder and stops. "Hey, Emma. Are you leaving already?"

"Yes."

"What happened to your date?"

"I dumped him. That was a blind date. I'm so sorry he was rude to you. I'm mortally embarrassed."

"Don't worry. I'm used to his kind."

"You shouldn't have to get used to it." I drop my eyes to his clothes. He's wearing a jacket and has his bag with him. "Where are you going?"

"My shift is over. I'm heading home. I have a finance exam I gotta study for."

Oh hell to the no. I'm not going to let this opportunity slip by. I need something good tonight to erase all memory of Scott the *Turd* from my head.

"I'm very good in finance," I say, turning on the flirtatious mode to the max.

Ricky's eyebrows arch at the same time a slow, knowing grin blossoms on his face. He laces his arm with mine, and we walk away from the restaurant together. When I realize he's steering me to the subway's entrance, I dig my feet into the ground and freeze.

"What's wrong?" He frowns.

"I can't take the metro."

"Why not?"

I don't answer for several beats. Instead, I keep staring at the stairs going down, which look like a giant gaping hole that wants to swallow me. Since that horrific day in Brussels, I haven't been able to go underground. Even riding regular trains is a struggle.

"Emma?"

"I-I suffer from claustrophobia," I lie. It's easier to tell people that than to admit out loud that I suffer from PSTD. I never talk about what happened with anyone besides my therapist.

"Oh. Is it really bad?"

Shit. Ricky's probably already second-guessing his decision to have me over. I spot a yellow cab approaching and raise my hand, flagging the car. Before Ricky can protest, I open the door and jump inside.

"Come on. I'll pay for the ride."

He slides in without looking in my direction and gives the driver his address. When he finally turns to me, his smile is less enthusiastic than before. I won't have that. Darkness is brewing in my chest and I need a distraction, so I slide my hand over his thigh and lean closer. "This is much cozier than the metro, don't you think?"

My fingers brush against his crotch, eliciting a hiss from him. "Yes," he replies with a gruff voice.

Oh yeah. We're back in business. I pull my hand away because giving a hand job in a taxi is a little too desperate. It's much more fun to tease and build expectation.

He laces his hand with mine and brings it to his lips. Goose bumps run up my arms. It's been a while since I hooked up with someone. We keep touching during the entire ride, but it's innocent: soft cheek caresses, thumb circling over the sensitive skin on the inside of my wrist. But once we arrive at our final destination and walk into his building, it's clear there won't be any studying tonight.

Ricky and I are already sucking each other's faces before he even gets the door to his apartment open. He kicks it closed again with a loud bang, then pushes me against the wall. His lips are at my neck while his left hand cups my breast through my clothes. His erection is pressing against my pelvis, and I know we won't spend much time with foreplay. That was the cab ride.

"Fuck, you taste so good," he whispers in my ear right before he cups my sex. I'm wet and so ready for this. But I want control, so I push him back toward the couch I spotted earlier.

"I hope you're ready for a private show," I whisper against his mouth before capturing his bottom lip between my teeth.

"You betcha."

"Good." I take a step back, giving him a little shove as I do. He falls on the couch and watches me with hooded eyes. My favorite type of look.

I reach for the zipper on the back of my skirt, ready to give him a little partial striptease, when I hear my phone ring in my purse. I have no desire to stop what I'm doing, though, so I ignore the noise and carry on. Once the zipper is lowered, I let it slip down to my feet. Ricky's eyes bulge when he catches sight of my Agent Provacateur panties. With desperate fingers, he unzips his jeans and sticks his hand into his underwear.

My phone rings again, a different tone this time. It gives me pause, and I look at my purse on the floor. That's Patricia's—my father's assistant—personal ringtone. She rarely calls me unless it's something urgent.

"What's wrong, Emma?" Ricky asks.

"I need to take this." I reach for my purse, fishing my phone out before it goes to voicemail. "Hello?"

"Oh, Em. I'm so glad I was able to reach you."

"What's wrong?"

"It's your father, hon. He had a heart attack."

My heart jumps up my throat just to immediately crash back down as heavy as lead. "What? When?"

"A little over an hour ago. He's in surgery now. You should get here as fast as you can. It's serious."

I get tunnel vision. The only thing important right now is to get my ass to the airport as fast as I can.

"I'll catch the first flight out." I end the call and pick up my skirt from the floor with the phone still in my hand.

"What's going on?" Ricky asks.

"It's my father. He suffered a heart attack. I have to go see him."

"Oh shit, Emma. I'm so sorry. Isn't he in California?"

"Yes." I make for the door without bothering to zip my skirt all the way up.

"Emma, wait. You forgot your coat." Ricky picks it up from where it landed when we came into the apartment. I don't even remember getting out of it.

I put it on as I walk out, not even thanking or saying goodbye to Ricky. He's already forgotten.

When I hit the pavement, I look frantically left and right, trying to spot a cab. There are none in sight, so I sprint toward the intersecting avenue, probably looking a little deranged running in my stilettos. When I turn a corner, I see a couple who has just flagged a cab down. Without pausing to think, I do something I've never done before—I cut in front of them and steal their ride, not even trying to apologize or explain it's an emergency. In true New York fashion, the driver doesn't give a rat's ass and drives off without a glance at the mad people cursing at me.

He asks where I'm headed and I tell him LaGuardia. Then he proceeds to talk my ear off, but I tune him out completely. There's only one single thought running through my head.

I can't lose Dad. He's the only person in the world who knows about all my flaws and still loves me. If he's gone—no, I can't think like that.

I won't lose him.

3

EMMA

February 2017, California

THE FLIGHT FROM NEW YORK CITY TO LA WAS THE LONGEST OF my life. I've never felt so impotent, so helpless, not even when I was hurt in the terrorist attack. Back then, I had been confused and lost. And I also had Declan there, offering me comfort.

I haven't thought about him in a long time, but today he's at the forefront of my mind. Maybe I should've tried to look for him, but in the whirlwind that followed my ordeal, I tried my best to distance myself from everything that reminded me of my darkest hour.

Strangely, I wish he were here with me now as I walk through these depressing hospital hallways. I called Patricia as soon as I landed, and she told me Dad was out of surgery already.

As soon as I turn a corner, I spot Dad's assistant sitting on a waiting chair in the hallway. *This is it.* My heart gets lodged in my throat, leaving my chest hollow.

Patricia stands when she sees me approach. Her eyes are

puffy and red, probably a stark contrast to mine since I haven't shed a single tear yet. I rarely cry; it does nothing to solve problems or make me feel better.

"Oh, Em," she says right before she engulfs me in a tight hug. Her flowery perfume reaches my nose, mixing with the sharp smell of ammonia that impregnates this place. I have to hold off a sneeze as I hug her back.

Stepping back, I ask, "How is he?

"The doctor says the surgery went well. It all depends on how he does during recovery."

"Is he allowed visitors?"

She nods, right before she pulls a tissue from her pocket and blows her nose. "I can't believe this happened. He didn't show any signs that he was unwell."

Patricia's voice trembles, and I can tell she's on the verge of waterworks again. Despite my resolve to remain strong, my heart clenches painfully and I feel a prickly sensation in my eyes. Grinding my teeth, I shove those feelings to a place where I can ignore them while cursing Patricia for bringing them forth. She's always been overly emotional.

Avoiding the window that lets me see into his room, I focus on the closed door instead. My palms are sweaty, and my mangled heart has once again lodged itself in my throat. I have to concentrate to draw air in and out.

Steeling myself, I push the door open, but the view of Dad in that hospital bed, hooked to machines, makes my legs go weak. He's only fifty-five, a man in his prime. I've always pictured him as larger than life, a fighter, but now, in that prone form and with sickly white skin, he looks like a ghost.

"Oh, Daddy," I whisper as I stop next to his bed.

He doesn't move, but I know he's breathing by the soft rise and fall of his chest and the constant, dull ping coming from the monitor. My eyes begin to burn, and when I rub them, I feel moisture in the corners. Damn it. I don't want to cry. If only I could ignore the pressure in my chest.

Dad's the only person I have left in this world. I don't remember when Mom died—I was too young—and my grandparents from both sides were gone before I was born.

I pull up a chair and sit as close as I can get to his bed. Curling my hand over his, I notice how cold it is.

"You got this, Daddy. We'll get through it together."

I DON'T REMEMBER FALLING ASLEEP, BUT I'M SUDDENLY JOLTED from my slumber when I hear Dad's raspy voice calling my name.

Blinking my eyes to clear them, I find Dad staring at me. "You're awake."

I feel a kink in my neck. That's what I get for sleeping in a chair.

"When did you get here, Em?"

"Early in the morning. I caught the first flight out of New York. How are you feeling?"

"Like I've been hit by an eighteen-wheeler." He fusses with his bed. "How does this damn thing work?"

"What do you need?"

"I want to sit up."

Dad fumbles with the bed's control, losing patience after a few seconds. He curses and frowns, just like he does whenever a client's getting on his nerves.

"Let me help you."

I pry the control from his hand and press the correct button. The back of the bed begins to lift. After a few seconds, I ask Dad if it's okay.

"Yes, it's fine, honey. Sorry for my grumpiness. I hate that you have to see me like this."

"It's okay, Daddy. You'll get out of here in no time."

"I hate hospitals. I always have. It reminds me too much of when I lost your mother and when I almost lost y—" He shakes his head. "I hate hospitals."

I drop my gaze as memories from those weeks Dad's referring to rush by. I try not to think too much of how I almost died or how hard those weeks were for him. I caught him crying like a baby once, but I pretended to be asleep. Just like me, he never shows weakness, and I wanted him to believe he'd never been caught.

"Your surgery went well. I can't wait to hear what the doctor has to say to you. I bet he'll give you a tongue lashing for not having healthier habits." I smirk, and Dad rolls his eyes.

"Oh yeah, I bet you'd love that. So, how's everything in New York?"

I shrug. "Not much to report. Work is good. MBA classes are kicking my butt, but it's nothing I can't handle."

"How was your date with Scott Fitzgerald the *Third*?"

My jaw drops. "How did you know I had a date with him?"

Dad chuckles, but his face twists into a grimace the next second. *Should he even be talking so much?*

"His father and I were fraternity brothers. He emailed me with the gossip." His voice is a little strained now.

"Dad, let's not waste time talking about that douchecanoe."

"I'm okay, honey. Talking distracts me. Anyway, I'm glad to hear the date didn't go well. I'd hate for our families to merge. The Fitzgeralds are all assholes."

Leaning back in my chair, I wave dismissively. "I don't have time for a relationship anyway. It's too much work, and they never last."

"Em, I don't like to hear you talk like that."

"Why not? It's the truth."

Dad's eyes dim a little as sadness takes over his features. "I know I haven't been a role model when it comes to relationships. I'm a divorce attorney who can't make his own marriages last, but sweetheart, that's not what I want for you. I want you to find happiness."

Frowning, I cross my arms. "Since when is the only way for a woman to be happy is tied to a man? I'm happy."

"I didn't say you need a man to be happy. But life is better when you find your person, somebody who gets you, who inspires you to be a better human being. Your mother was the one for me."

Dad's never spoken about Mom before, not like this. I assumed he would've ended up divorcing her just like the others if she hadn't died. Hearing him talk about her with such reverence hurts my heart. Believing she wasn't special to him made it easier to bear her absence.

"I'm not immortal," he continues, his voice a little choked up. "I don't want to depart this plane without knowing you won't be alone."

A lonely tear escapes my eye and I hastily wipe it off. "I don't think I can ever feel that way about anyone, Daddy. Maybe I'm broken."

"No, you're not broken. And I don't believe you can't fall in love. I see the way you are with your friends. You're loyal, kind, and you love them deeply. You can fall in love, honey."

I stare at my lap, thinking about all my past relationships, as brief as they were. In the beginning, I did feel the high, the butterflies in my stomach, until fear replaced those feelings and my walls went back up again. I never really gave any of those guys a chance.

My hand goes immediately to my side, pressing against the jagged scar that now adorns my torso. Declan's image comes to mind again. We shared something powerful that day. He saved my life. If there's anyone in this world who can be the one for me, he has a fighting chance.

"Promise me you'll try, Em," Dad continues, bringing me back from my thoughts.

I grab his hand and squeeze lightly. "I promise, Daddy."

Now I just have to go find the man.

4

—

RORI

For fuck's sake. Why must my house phone always ring when I'm in the middle of something?

Cursing, I turn off the shower and dash out of the bathroom, soaking wet, leaving a wet trail behind me. Only my family has this phone number, so it's not like I can ignore it.

I pull the yellowed receiver from its base on the wall with a jerky movement. "Hello?"

"Finally. Why do you always take forever to answer the bloody phone, brother?"

"I was taking a shower, Keira," I say through clenched teeth. "What's the emergency?"

"Oh, no emergency—"

"Keira, how many times have I told you not to call this number unless someone's dying?" Phone still in hand, I look for a towel. The device is mounted to the wall that opens to the arched entry leading to the kitchen, but today there's no dishtowel in sight.

"I called your mobile phone first. Stop being a grump. I have news."

"Did Clemmot finally get tired of you and dump your ass?"

"You're such a whanker, Rori. He didn't dump me. He proposed!" She screams so loudly, I have to pull the receiver away from my ear or risk going deaf.

"Congratulations, sis. Where're Mum and Dad? At church, on their knees saying thanks to the Lord for this miracle?" I chuckle.

"Fuck off." Keira's stern tone has a hint of humor in it. This is what we do, pick on each other until someone breaks down and cries. Granted, that hasn't happened in over fifteen years, but it's still fun to try.

Tired of dripping water on the wooden floor, I tell Keira to hold on while I get a towel from the bathroom. The excess of water in my long hair is what's annoying me the most. Actually, I'm tired of the whole bloody lot. Maybe it's time to shave it off.

Now with towel in hand, I ask the dreadful question. "So, when's the big day?"

"Please don't hate me. It's March 18th, and you'd better be here."

"What? Are you out of your mind? Why the rush?"

"Claude got offered a new job overseas, in Australia actually, and we want to be married before we relocate to the other side of the world. You'll come, right, Rori? You *must* come."

I pinch the bridge of my nose, already imagining the pandemonium life must be right now at the O'Shea house. "It's going to be hard, Keira. I run a pub, in case you've forgotten."

"Exactly. You're the boss. You can do as you please."

I shake my head even though Keira can't see the gesture. My sister's always been a little out of touch with reality. "I can't do as I please. I gotta make sure the pub is staffed for the duration of my absence, for starters."

"Isn't that what the manager's for?"

"*I'm* the manager."

"Maybe it's high time you consider hiring an assistant, at least. When was the last time you had a vacation?"

Clenching my jaw, I lean against the wall and stare at nothing. I haven't taken time off since I inherited the pub five years ago. I'm due for a break, but Ireland isn't on the top of my list, even as much as I miss my family.

"You haven't been home in six years, Rori," Keira continues. "Nobody cares anymore about the accid—"

"For fuck's sake, Keira. I haven't thought about that in years."

"Then why haven't you come to visit? You know Mum hates to travel."

My shoulders sag forward as I let out a heavy sigh. Guilt mixes with my irritation. I wasn't lying before. I haven't really dwelled in the past thanks to the pub Uncle George left me. It kept me busy enough. But the idea of returning to the place I grew up, seeing all those familiar faces and reading pity in their eyes, makes me want to barf.

"It's not like I have a bloody choice now, is it?" I bark like a fearful mutt who finds himself cornered.

"It would be brilliant if you didn't consider coming to your sister's wedding a death sentence. But if it's such a burden, *Rori Galahad O'Shea*, then don't come. It wasn't like Mum was more excited by the prospect of your imminent visit than by her own daughter's engagement."

I open my mouth to reply, but Keira hangs up before I can. She always needs to have the last word. Irritated, I return the receiver to its hook using more force than necessary. One of these days, I'll just rip the stupid thing off the wall and break it to pieces.

Pulling at my hair, I stride back to my bedroom, trying hard not to fall for Keira's guilt trip. Impossible. My chest is already heavy. Distracted, I end up tripping over my running shoes, which I left in the middle of the room this morning. By a miracle, I don't fall flat on my face. With a roar, I kick one of them hard. It hits the middle of the bookshelf, knocking some of my books and picture frames to the floor.

Goddamn it!

Breathing hard, I stare at the mess I made. I haven't felt this rage since that dreadful day out in the rain nine years ago. Shit. Maybe I'm not over it.

I bend over to collect the fallen books when a picture slips out of one. It's facedown, but the handwriting and date on the back tell me exactly who's in it—the other side of my misfortune. Without looking at it, I shove it back in the book and return it to the shelf.

One day I'll be able to get rid of it. Maybe on the same day I look at my scars and don't wish for a do-over.

5

—————

EMMA

MY HEART IS HEAVY WHEN I LEAVE THE HOSPITAL. I WANTED TO stay, but the doctor kicked me out of the room, saying visiting hours were over. I should go home and change, but the idea of being alone right now just makes me more depressed. I ask the Uber driver to take me to one of my favorite spots, Manhattan Beach. The Pacific Ocean is one of the things I missed the most about California.

During the drive, my thoughts wander back to Declan and inevitably to that terrifying day in Brussels. I never allowed myself to think about him because the memory always came with the trauma. I wonder if he's also assaulted by vivid nightmares, or if he can't bear to go underground just like I can't. My therapist said meeting him again might help heal my emotional wound for good, but I've ignored her. Now I'm willing to take the risk. I made a promise to Dad, and I never back down on my word. If finding my soul mate is going to give my father peace of mind, then I need to go for the person with the highest chance of being my match, as crazy as it sounds.

The Uber driver announces we've arrived, bringing me back to the here and now. We're in front of a popular restaurant

—the address I inserted in the app. I look out the window and hesitate. It's past one in the afternoon, and the place is full of happy shiny people. Not exactly where I want to be, but I thank the driver and get out. Two guys sitting on a table outside turn and look at me. One of them smirks, but I can't tell if he's amused because I look like hell or it's because he's checking me out. It doesn't really matter; I'm not going in to find out.

Turning on my heels, I veer toward the beach. The sun is out in full force, which means everyone in the neighborhood decided to come here. The oceanic walkway is as busy as ever, with a mix of joggers, parents with strollers, and tourists. I continue toward the beach, longing to sink my feet into the sand, to feel the warm texture between my toes. I take off my shoes and walk without direction, succeeding on blocking out the crowd's noise. Losing track of time is easy, and only when my stomach grumbles do I notice where I am. I'm already in Hermosa Beach, close to the main promenade.

Without bothering to put my shoes back on, I continue barefoot to a place I haven't been in ages, the pub where Wreck of the Day used to play before they skyrocketed to fame. All tables outside are taken, but inside it's a little calmer. I spot an empty booth all the way in the back and make a beeline for it.

I'm hungry but I don't want to eat, so when the waitress comes by, I just order a glass of whiskey, neat. She returns with my drink and a bowl of peanuts minutes later. I had every intention to nurse my drink, but I end up gulping it down before she has the chance to leave.

"Bring me another one, please." I offer her my empty glass.

She frowns, emphasizing the lines on her forehead. Her flattened lips indicate disapproval as her eyes drop to the clothes I'm wearing.

"Would you like to order something to eat?" she asks.

"No. Just the drink, and make it a double this time."

Making a clicking sound with her tongue, she turns around.

I can only imagine the judgmental thoughts running through her head. I bet if I were a guy, she wouldn't even blink. Or maybe she'd shove her cleavage in my face and flirt with me. Double standards all around.

I pull out my phone and type 'Declan Kelly' in the Facebook search bar. A list of profiles pops up, but none are his. I move my search to Google, which turns out to be even more frustrating. The sound of glass hitting hard wood in front of me jars me from my thoughts. No 'there you are' or any type of finesse this time from my stick-up-her-butt waitress. We'll see how she'll react when she gets no tip. *Bitch.*

I take a large gulp of my drink but don't finish it right away, too busy on my detective work. Now that I've decided to locate Declan, it's more than a mission—it's a challenge, and I can never turn away from one. It would be easier to hire a professional, but what's the fun in that?

A text message pops up on my screen, from my coworker Femke. She heard about my fiasco date with Scott the *Turd.* Only, instead of apologizing for setting me up with a dud, she's upset that I've embarrassed her. *Are you fucking kidding me?* My fingers type faster than I can think, annoyance and whiskey erasing my usual diplomatic approach.

Femke's response is swift. **That was extremely unprofessional, Emma.** I scroll up to read what I wrote. *Hmm, I guess my reference to Scott's tiny dick was probably too much. Too late now.*

I push the phone aside, making sure the screen is facedown, and rest my head in my hands. My chest is heavy again, and a huge lump forms in my throat. Fuck. Is this the prelude of the biggest meltdown I've had since elementary school? Not if I can help it.

I raise my head and try to find my sourpuss waitress in the crowd. The pub is busier now, but I make eye contact with her after a moment. I know she's seen my raised hand, but instead of coming to my table, she turns to the bar.

That's when I see the sexy owner is here. Shit, I can't believe I missed him when I arrived. I've only met him once, when I came here with my roommates, Saylor and Liv. A bolt of excitement rushes through my veins, but then I remember that I'm on a mission to find another man, and the little spark dies.

It's hard not to notice how good-looking the guy is, though. His long hair is pulled back into a bun, and his strong jaw is framed by dark blond scruff. The dark T-shirt he's wearing does little to hide the bulge of his impressive arms and wide chest. He's the epitome of roguishly sexy.

The waitress leans over the counter and whispers in the guy's ear. He glances in my direction with a frown, immediately putting me on the defensive. Sure as shit, he gets rid of the small towel over his shoulder—the one all bartenders in the world seem to wear—and walks around the bar, heading in my direction. My back stiffens and I clench my jaw. Some of the female patrons turn to admire his frame, and I confess my heart is hammering a little faster inside my chest.

He stops in front of my table, and I have to raise my chin to stare into his eyes. I can't tell the exact color—they could be hazel or warm brown—but they're intense. A shiver runs down my spine. He doesn't say a word for several beats, and my hands start to sweat. I should say something, I'm really good with words, but I find myself tongue-tied.

He slides in the booth with me, leaving a gap between our bodies, and rests his elbows on the table. "What's the problem?"

My jaw slackens, his impatient tone catching me off-guard. No 'hello.' No 'how are you.' There are so many things I want to say to him, but none of my retorts seem appropriate.

"I don't know what you mean." I curl my hand tighter around the empty glass.

"No one comes into a pub barefoot, wearing last night's

clothes, and proceeds to order booze if they don't have a problem. So what is it, Emma?"

I let go of the glass as my back hits the booth. "You know my name?"

His eyes widen a fraction, and he seems to be contemplating his answer. After several beats, he replies, "We were introduced before. You used to be Saylor's roommate."

Oh, so he does remember the night I came. Saylor used to come by every week, but due to my busy schedule, I only came once. A little warmth spreads through my chest, even if it's silly to feel giddy that the guy remembers my name.

"I'm extremely good with names and faces," he continues.

And just like that, the sentiment evaporates. Here I was thinking he remembered me because he *saw* me.

With stiff back and a glower, I say, "You're right, I *do* have a problem. It's with the terrible service in this place. You really ought to raise the bar when it comes to hiring staff. Your waitress was rude as shit."

He narrows his eyes, and I notice a vein on his forehead throb. Seconds tick by with both of us glaring at each other.

"Out of courtesy to my friendship with Saylor, I won't ask you to leave. But if you want to stay and drown your sorrows in alcohol, you must eat. I won't have you puking all over the place. I'll put in an order of fish and chips for you. It's the best in Hermosa Beach."

He slides out of the booth and walks away, leaving me no chance to argue. He's going to *let* me stay? What an arrogant ass. Maybe I should leave, but pride keeps my ass glued to the seat. I'll prove to him that I can drink and not make a fool out of myself.

Avoiding looking in his direction, I continue my online manhunt and fifteen minutes later, a large plate of fish and chips appears in front of me. I lift my face to glower at the waitress, but it's the grouchy owner who serves me.

I just realized I can't remember his name. I think it starts with an *R*. Roger? Ray? Rori? I'm not going to ask, though.

My stomach decides it's the time to rumble loudly. Shoot me. I bet the entire restaurant heard it. The guy doesn't say a word, but there's a victorious smirk on his lips before he walks away.

Jerkface.

I try one of the fries and almost moan out loud. It's so good, salty and crunchy. In no time I polish off the dish, feeling tremendously better with a full belly. But my glass is empty and the heaviness in my chest is still there, so I order another double whiskey, hoping it'll finally do the trick of dulling the constant ache.

Eventually, nature calls, and as I slide out of the booth, I realize hours must've passed. The place is absolutely packed. I can't believe I didn't notice the change and the noise. I walk by a long table occupied by a group of college guys. They whistle and make stupid comments about me, the usual type of douchery you can expect from drunk jerks like them. Despite my carefree nature when it comes to relationships, nothing turns me off more than idiots like them.

Inside the bathroom, I try not to wince at my reflection in the mirror. I'm wearing zero makeup, my lack of sleep is showing in dark circles under my eyes, and my hair is dull and lifeless. My outfit is so wrinkled, it looks like it just came out of the washer. I don't know what those guys were looking at. I've never felt more unsexy in my entire life.

On the way back to my table, I try to smooth the lines in my top, knowing it's futile. I stop abruptly when I see my way is blocked by someone wearing bright-colored sneakers. The hallway leading to the restrooms is narrow, but not that narrow. Irritated, I look up and find one of the college guys smiling at me.

"Where are you going in such a hurry, babe?"

Wrinkling my nose, I step back, the smell of beer almost making me gag. "None of your business."

"Back to your empty table? What happened, babe? Got stood up?" He moves closer, sneering at me in a leery way.

My hand automatically moves to my purse only to remember that I left it back at my table. *Fuck. No pepper spray.*

"I'm not your *babe*. Now move out of my way, asshole."

I shouldn't be so confrontational, but truth is, I've been exposed to too many fuckers in the last forty-eight hours. I'm at my limit. But my reply was clearly the wrong thing to say. His face twists into an angry scowl, and I find myself pushed against the wall while his beefy hands curl around my biceps.

"Who are you calling asshole, bitch?"

"Let go of me." I struggle against his hold, a second away from screaming at the top of my lungs.

He ignores me and moves closer instead. Before he can trap me for good, I stomp hard on his instep, which makes him howl like the animal he is. In retaliation, he pushes me and I hit my head on the corner of a console table nearby. Pain explodes in my forehead just before I hit the sticky floor.

The room begins to spin, and I have trouble focusing on anything. Leaning on my elbow, I touch the sore spot and feel moisture there. There's a scuffle, and I hear the guy yell at someone. I have to squint to see what's going on. When my vision finally returns to normal, I catch sight of the owner locking the guy's arms behind his back and escorting him out.

"Are you okay?" the waitress who was serving my table asks. It seems she also came to the rescue.

"I'm fine."

She helps me up, then looks at my forehead with eyebrows furrowed. "You're bleeding. Let's get you cleaned up."

I let her lead me back to the busy pub. Some heads turn our way, probably those who noticed the owner taking the trash out. The table where those assholes were sitting is now empty. I veer for my booth to grab my purse, and then we continue down another narrow hallway. The waitress stops in front of a closed door. She pulls out a key from her apron's pocket and swings the door open, revealing a narrow staircase.

"What's up there?"

"Rori's apartment. It's were the first aid kit is."

Ah, so I was right. His name does begin with an *R*.

Despite my current situation, a thrill of excitement rushes through me. You can usually learn a lot about someone by how they live. I'm not sure why I'm so curious about Rori, but I am.

The front door opens to a small living room where a brown, comfy-looking couch takes center stage—and most of the space. A reclaimed wooden crate serves as the coffee table and on top, a few magazines lie scattered. Upon closer inspection, I realize they aren't magazines but business catalogues.

A small open kitchen is on the right side of the living room, a counter that also serves as an eating table separating the two rooms.

"Please sit down while I get the first aid kit."

"Okay. Hmm, I don't know your name."

"It's Lena. I'll be right back."

The woman disappears down the hallway, and I get a little jealous that she's free to roam Rori's apartment like that. Maybe she's his girlfriend. The thought makes me nauseous, but why? Who knows? Maybe I hit my head too hard.

I hear her let out a string of curses right before she returns to the living room carrying a white plastic box. Her lips are nothing more than a thin, flat line.

"What's wrong?" I ask.

"I shouldn't have trusted Rori to actually have a stocked first aid kit. Why are guys so bad at domestic stuff?"

"Why didn't you take care of it?"

Lena raises both eyebrows. "Why would I do that? I'm a waitress, not his housekeeper." She sets the box on the table and heads to the door. "I think we have Band-Aids in the office. I'll be right back. Why don't you get cleaned up? The bathroom is down the hall, first door to your right."

She disappears again, leaving me alone in her boss's apartment. I get hit with a crazy impulse to inspect everything, to look in every nook for clues about the rugged man downstairs. But I fight the urge—I'm not a nutcase, after all. Instead, I head to the bathroom, taking the first aid kit with me. It's tiny, not much bigger than a broom closet, with barely enough space for the shower, toilet, and sink. I'm not sure how such a big guy like Rori can maneuver here. Above the sink, a skinny cabinet doubles as a mirror. As much I don't want to be a nosy person, I do look inside.

I don't find anything unusual, just basic painkillers and antacid shit. I shut the cabinet and get on with the task at hand. Narrowing my eyes, I inspect the gash just over my right eyebrow. It's not that big, so I don't think I need to make a trip to the emergency room.

Looking inside the first aid kit, I get why Lena was cursing. There's not much there, but I do find gauze and hydrogen peroxide. I wince at the sting as I wipe the blood off. Dizziness threatens to take over me, so I finish as quickly as possible.

When I return to the living room, there's still no sign of Lena. I could just head back down to the restaurant, but the weariness of the day has finally caught up with me, and that couch is looking mighty inviting. I sit down and grab my phone, thinking I can just return to my search.

At least that's my intention—not to fall asleep within the minute.

6
____

RORI

M**Y BLOOD IS STILL PUMPING HARD IN MY VEINS WHEN** I **RETURN** to the pub after throwing out those scumbags. I knew they'd be trouble the moment they walked in with their cocky attitude and loud mouths. I was already prepared to ask them to leave before I heard the scuffle near the restrooms. It took a Herculean effort not to beat that asshole into a pulp once I saw what he'd done to Emma.

I search for Saylor's friend, but there's a family occupying her table now. I turn to Jack, the busboy, when he walks by. "Have you seen Lena?"

"I think she took that chick to your apartment. She was bleeding."

Fuck.

I try not to show my concern as I stride through the pub. I don't need my patrons thinking something's wrong. It was bad enough that I had to kick those assholes out.

I have the door that leads to my apartment half open when Lena reappears, coming from the back office.

"Where is she?"

"Upstairs."

"You left a stranger alone in my apartment?"

Lena narrows her eyes. "I thought she was Saylor's friend." She shoves a box of Band-Aids into my hands. "Here. Keep your first aid kit stocked next time."

She turns on her heels with a humph and resumes her shift. Lena's worked at Closing Time since the place still belonged to my uncle. She trained me when I started and treated me like I was her own child. It's why I put up with her attitude. I would've made her a manager if she wanted the job, but she claimed she'd make more money in tips and didn't need the extra stress.

Grumbling, I take the stairs two steps at a time, but once I stop in front of my door, I pause and take a deep breath. Emma's presence in the pub was an unwelcome surprise. After we met, I'd hoped to never see her again. But then Saylor came in one day with the girl in tow. I wasn't happy to learn they were roommates, but since Emma didn't show any indication that she remembered me, I decided not to bring it up.

Despite not having the best impression of her, that didn't stop me from trying to know more. She's most definitely a spoiled rich girl who likes to party, the kind of woman I tend to veer away from. But for whatever reason, she intrigues me. Since the first time we met, I've felt an odd pull toward her, a curiosity, and it unnerved me. She's trouble with a capital *T*. Seeing her do the walk of shame into my pub today only served to aggravate my already sour mood.

I push the door open with every intention to keep my annoyance in check, but I'm not prepared to find the woman sound asleep on my couch. She has one arm folded close to her body, her head resting on her hand. Her skirt is hiked up, showing off toned legs that make my blood pump faster. I pull my gaze away and rub my face.

Shit, what now?

Walking slowly to avoid making any noise, I approach Emma and crouch in front of her. The small gash on her eyebrow is clean and no longer bleeding. It was only a superficial cut. My eyes roam over her face, taking in every single detail. Jesus, she's stunning. High cheekbones, natural eyelashes that go on for miles, and perfect Cupid's bow lips. I never allowed myself to look too closely at her before, which turned out to be the right decision, because I'm having a hard time looking away now. Her skin is a little pale and there are dark circles under her eyes. My guess is she was up last night until late. No wonder she crashed. I'm torn between waking her up to send her away and letting her stay here.

Something flashes on the floor—her phone. She must've dropped it when she fell asleep. I pick it up and see the text message on the screen. Reading it is unavoidable. It's from a woman named Patricia, telling Emma to stay home tonight and rest since visiting hours at the hospital are over.

Ah, fuck. Now I feel like an ass. It seems Emma wasn't partying last night after all. Mum always warned me not to assume things. I place the phone on the coffee table and go in search of a blanket. No way in hell I'm waking her up now.

When I return with blanket in hand, she turns, making her top slide up. I freeze when I see a long, jagged scar marring her otherwise smooth skin. I'm not a doctor, but that looks like an almost deadly wound.

What happened to you, Emma?

My chest is a little heavier with guilt as I place the soft blanket over her. She stirs but doesn't wake up. I don't move from my spot, just keep staring at her while a myriad of thoughts bounce around in my head. There are too many for me to make any sense of them. Only one thing is certain: contempt is no longer the prevailing emotion. Curiosity is, and I know if given the chance, I'm going down the rabbit hole.

I'm a glutton for punishment.

Emma

My eyes fly open and darkness greets me. *Where the hell am I?* My face is pressed against a leather texture, probably a couch, and since I don't own a leather couch, I know I'm not home.

Fuck. What did I do?

I roll my body too fast and end up falling on the floor with a loud thud. "Ouch."

Suddenly, a bit of illumination pours through the crack of the door ahead and clues me in where I am. *I'm still in Rori's apartment. Shit.* The door opens and out comes the man himself, wearing nothing more than a pair of loose sweatpants.

Dear baby Jesus. The guy is sculpted perfection. Even in the semidarkness, I can see that his abs are the stuff of dreams.

"Are you okay there?" He crouches in front of me and helps me get up. My face feels hot, and I'm glad there's not a lot of light.

"Yes. I fell off the couch."

"I noticed." He doesn't move, still holding my arm. I actually like the proximity.

"I'm so sorry I fell asleep. You should've woken me."

"Nah, you looked like you needed the rest." Rori finally lets go, taking a step back. He looks away and runs a hand through his unbound, glorious hair. Oh my Lord. He's like a modern-day Tarzan, and I wish I was his Jane.

No, Emma. Focus. You don't have time to get sidetracked. You need to find your Prince Charming, and his name is Declan.

"What time is it?" I ask, more to fill the silence as I bend over to check my phone.

"A little past four in the morning," he says.

"What? Oh my God. I have to leave." I unlock my phone

and immediately see I've received a text from Patricia. My heart hammers inside of my chest faster than a hummingbird bats its wings. *Did Dad get worse while I was sleeping?*

"Are you sure? You can stay here until morning. It's not a big deal."

I shake my head. "I have to be somewhere."

Patricia's message only says I should stay home to rest. I release the breath I was holding.

"The hospital?" Rori asks, surprising me.

I snap my face to his. "How did you...? Wait, did you read the message on my phone?"

"By accident. It was flashing on the screen when I picked it up from the floor."

I have no reason to doubt Rori, but I'm still annoyed.

"Well, just because they say visiting hours are over doesn't mean I can't try."

"Usually hospitals are pretty strict with their rules."

Frowning, I level him with a glare. "What's it to you, anyway? I thought you didn't like me. As matter of fact, you were ready to kick me out of your pub not too long ago."

Rori's eyebrows rise and I sense a shift in his attitude. "Only because I thought you would cause a scene."

"What? That's ridiculous. So now a grown woman can't walk into a pub and order a real drink without people immediately assuming she's a troublemaker?"

Rori turns his back to me and flips on the light. The sudden glare hurts my eyes, and I raise my arm to shield them from it. I can still see Rori through the barrier and immediately notice when his gaze drops to my midriff. *Oh shit, is my skin exposed?* I drop my arm fast. "What are you looking at?"

A hint of guilt shines in his eyes when his gaze collides with mine. "Nothing."

Bullshit. He must've seen my scar. I could confront him or

get the hell out of here. I choose the latter. "Where's my purse?" I quickly scan the living room without luck.

Rori walks to the front door and grabs my purse, which was hanging from a hook near the coatrack. I get even more irritated that the guy looks sexy as hell even in the middle of the night, whereas I must look like shit. His hair isn't even tangled. I never slept with a guy with long hair before. It would be a nice change of pace, pulling his hair during sex rather than the other way around.

Ugh! Stop thinking about screwing the guy, Emma. Gee, it's like I have no self-control.

With a jerky movement, I pull the bag from his hand. But because the world is out to get me today, the purse opens, spilling all its contents onto the floor.

"Crap!"

I get on my knees and hastily try to put everything back, and Rori does the same. He clears his throat when he grabs my sparkly bullet. I don't even know why that thing was in there. Will the humiliation ever end? It's not that I'm ashamed of my sex toys, but I definitely don't want Rori of all people to know I carry them in my bag. He already thinks I'm a wild girl.

I wish the floor would open up and swallow me whole. My face is most definitely red now; I don't need to see myself in the mirror to know that. I yank the device from him and shove it in my bag before he can make any comment about it. He doesn't, thank God. I avoid eye contact just the same.

"Do you need a ride home?"

"No!" I blurt out, looking at him just in time to catch his wince. I soften my tone. "I mean, there's no need. I'll call an Uber."

"Are you sure?"

"Yes." I make my way to the door but sense him following me, so I look over my shoulder. "Seriously, Rori. I don't need a ride."

"I got that, but I still need to unlock the pub door for you."

"Oh. Right." I move out of the way and let him go first. I don't want him walking behind me; it would give him the chance to watch me and judge me even more.

"So, there's only one way out of this apartment?"

"Yeah. This wasn't a living area originally, just extra storage space for the pub. My uncle converted it into a studio for the nights he was too tired to drive home."

"Your uncle? So this place belongs to him?"

"Used to. He passed away five years ago and left it to me."

"I'm sorry."

The subject makes me inevitably think about Dad, and the momentarily forgotten worry comes back with a vengeance. Rori opens the door leading to the pub, and the smell of beer and fried food reaches my nose. I didn't notice it before, but now that the place is dark and empty, it's all I can smell.

Rori punches a code for the alarm, then unlocks the door. The previously busy promenade is deserted, and now I can hear the sound of the ocean clearly. I take a deep breath when I step outside, then look at Rori, who's watching me from the door. I can't read his expression, but something about his demeanor makes my heart do a backflip. It almost feels like déjà vu.

"You don't need to wait with me. I'll be fine."

"You're out of your mind if you think I'll let you wait here in the middle of the night alone."

I pull the pepper spray canister from my bag. "I'm covered."

He scoffs. "Right. Like you were covered earlier when that asshole assaulted you."

His comment makes me bristle, and I go on the defensive. "I didn't think I'd need protection in *your* establishment."

Rori shakes his head and drops his gaze to his feet. "I'm sorry. And you're right, you shouldn't need protection here."

His regretful tone mollifies me. "Don't beat yourself up over it. Assholes are everywhere. You can't control what people do."

He looks up without replying to my comment. Seconds go by in silence while he keeps staring. I wish I knew what he's thinking. *He's probably wondering why you haven't called the Uber yet, silly.* I get on with it, and the app tells me the closest driver will be here in ten minutes.

Shit. Ten minutes to come up with inane topics to fill the uncomfortable silence.

"Do you like living in California?" I ask.

"Yeah, I do."

"But you don't miss Ireland?"

"Sometimes."

"When was the last time you visited?"

"It's been a while."

I bite my lower lip. *This isn't going anywhere. Maybe I should just shut up and play with my phone.*

"Have you ever been to Ireland?" he asks.

"Yeah, a few years ago with my father."

"Is he the one in the hospital?"

"Yeah." I turn away, hating how my voice sounds so choked up.

"I'm truly sorry, Emma. What happened, if you don't mind me asking?"

"Heart attack. He got lucky this time."

"I'm sorry about my behavior earlier. I misjudged you, and I truly regret it. I didn't know."

With a smirk, I reply, "You thought I was a hungover chick doing the walk of shame, didn't you?"

He stares hard, his eyes squinting a little, as if he's thinking how to best reply. Even with the distance, I can feel the intensity of this gaze.

"Something like that," he replies after a while, his voice low and husky.

The sound makes my legs a little unsteady, but the words erase the fake smile from my face. "You're not the first one to judge me, and you won't be the last."

"That doesn't bother you?"

"No," I lie. "I can't control what people think about me. If I start living my life trying to please others, what kind of life would that be?"

Rori doesn't answer and, after a moment, I feel the need to add, "It doesn't matter, anyway. My days being Dona Juanita are over."

"Dona Juanita?" he chuckles.

"Dona Juanita, man-eater. It's better than being called a slut. Anyway, I made a promise to my father that I'd give a serious relationship a try. He's afraid to die and leave me all alone."

"Oh." Rori sounds surprised.

"You think that's a terrible idea?"

"No. I just... well, you can't force these things."

"Trust me, I know. But I have a plan."

He crosses his arms in front of his naked chest, and I kind lose track of my thoughts. *Would it kill him to put a T-shirt on?*

"Care to share?" he asks.

"I, uh.... There's someone I met last year who I shared a very powerful moment with. I'm going to find him."

"It sounds like you have everything figured out." There's sarcasm in his tone, but also irritation. Why would he care?

"Not really. For starters, I can't find him anywhere on social media, and searching the place where he's from didn't help either."

"Okay, now I'm intrigued. Where's the lucky guy from?"

"Your side of the pond. Kinsale, Ireland."

Rori uncrosses his arms and straightens his back. "That's where I'm from."

Wait, what? No, that's too much of a coincidence. He must be pulling my leg.

"Ha-ha, very funny, Rori."

"I'm serious."

There's no hint of mischief in his gaze or in his facial expression. If he's lying, he's very good at it. I take an eager step in his direction. "Maybe you know him."

"Maybe." He shrugs. "What's his name?"

"Declan Kelly."

Rori stares in silence without blinking. It's almost like he wants to prolong the suspense on purpose.

"I'm sorry. I don't know anyone by that name."

And just like that, my excitement deflates. "That's okay. It was a long shot. I'll just fly there and look for the guy myself."

"Are you that determined to find a stranger?"

"Yes."

Another pause where Rori seems to be evaluating me. He really needs to stop doing that.

"I have a proposition for you," he says.

"What kind of proposition?"

"It happens that my older sister is getting married in a month. If you agree to be my plus one at her wedding, I'll help you find your guy."

I try not to get overexcited by the idea, only because the prospect of traveling with Rori is more enticing than finding Declan. So I force my jets to cool off.

"Why do you need a plus one?"

"I haven't been home in a long time, and I could use a buffer. I promise to keep things utterly platonic. You don't need to pretend you're my girlfriend."

Hmm, it's not a bad deal. There are definitely more pros than cons. I don't think Rori has ulterior motives, even though I know he's not telling me the whole truth.

Oh, what the hell.

I breach the distance between us and offer him my hand. Rori drops his gaze for a split second, then looks into my eyes. They're dark and enigmatic, but they have a pull on me nonetheless. He finally accepts the handshake, covering my hand with his much bigger one. My heart decides to go into overdrive, not because of the handshake but because of the dazzling smile he grants me.

Oh boy. This trip will be a challenge, in more ways than one.

7

———

RORI

March 2017, California

"Mum! Rori's bringing a friend to the wedding!" my little sister Lizzy shouts on the phone, right into my ear, making me regret telling her.

In the background, I hear my mother reply, but I can't make out her words. A second later, Lizzy's happy to provide that information.

"Mum says she can't make special arrangements last minute. The house will be at full capacity, you know?"

Rubbing my face, I lean against the wall and look in the window's direction. "I'm staying at a hotel."

"What? No. You haven't been home in so long. Mum will be crushed."

"You just said there's no room in the house."

"Yes there is. Mum's being overly dramatic. You can take the pullout couch in Dad's office if you don't mind sharing it with your friend. Is he hot?"

"It's not a guy."

"Wait, you're bringing a *girlfriend*?"

"Lizzy, don't get overexcited. She's just a friend."

"Blimey. I'll tell Mum. She's already freaking out. When do you get here?"

"Not until Sunday. We're spending the night in Dublin tomorrow."

"I'm jealous. I don't get to do *anything*."

I chuckle. In the six years I've been away, Lizzy hasn't changed a bit. She was always a bit whiny, the baby of the family through and through.

My chest feels a little heavy. I've missed so much of her growing up. When I came to California nine years ago, she was only seven.

"Listen, I have to go now or I'll miss my flight. I'll see you soon, Lizzy."

"Have a safe trip."

After ending the call, I shove my phone into my jacket pocket and do a final scan of my living room to make sure I didn't forget anything before hoisting my duffel bag over my shoulder. My backpack and the garment bag with my suit are hanging by the door on the coatrack. I pull my passport out, taking a deep breath as I do. The last time I was home, things weren't great. I almost lapsed into the mess I was when my parents sent me to live with my uncle.

Apprehension makes my stomach tie into knots. Just knowing that in twenty-four hours I'll be back to the place I grew up in brings me back to the exact moment when my life derailed completely. I curl my hands into fists and fight the darkness I already feel swirling in my chest.

My phone vibrates in my pocket, distracting me from my thoughts. It's a text from Emma. After she spent half the night in my apartment a month ago, we met a few times to hash out the details of our trip together. We're on the same flight, but I refused her offer to pay for an upgrade to business class.

Hurry up or we'll miss our flight, the message reads.

What? With a groan, I text her back, asking if she's waiting for me outside. I told her I'd meet her at the airport.

Instead of replying, she calls.

"Yes, I'm outside," she says by way of greeting. "There's no need for you to pay for a cab when I'd already gotten a car. Now come on. What's taking you so long?"

"I'll be right down." I end the call before she can offer a reply, thinking I need to set her straight before we board the plane. That's what I get for breaking my own rules. I had to go and offer to play guide for her in Ireland. Hopefully she'll keep me distracted enough that depression can't find me.

It didn't take long for me to notice Emma's bossy tendencies. She's stubborn and decisive, but she has a huge problem—she never accepts the word no. She takes everything as a challenge. Those are qualities I usually appreciate, but not when it goes against what *I* want.

I find her waiting for me just outside of the pub. She's leaning against the front wall with arms folded, looking out into the distance. Her left foot is propped against the wall, emphasizing her toned legs even more. She's not wearing yoga pants like a lot of girls do when traveling, but her skintight jeans are just as revealing. Fuck me. I can't allow myself to develop any sort of emotions for her. I've agreed to help her find another bloke, for crying out loud.

Just remember the first night you met her, Rori.

She glances in my direction and smiles from ear to ear, making my heart pound faster. "Ready?"

"I told you I didn't need a ride," I grumble.

Dismissing my comment with a wave, she turns toward the main street. My eyes involuntarily drop to her ass. It's a nice ass, round and firm. I begin to imagine what kind of underwear she has on, but stop when my dick stirs in my pants. I can't go there. I bring my gaze up and notice her hair is lighter, and also a little shorter.

"I like your hair."

Shit, what am I? A teen girl? I sound like Lizzy.

Without missing a step, Emma glances over her shoulder. "Thanks. I figured I'd upgrade my looks for this trip."

Jealousy comes out of nowhere, spearing my chest with an ice-cold dagger. "For Declan," I say while curling my hand tighter around the garment bag's hanger.

"No, for me." She stops next to a black Escalade parked by the curb, and a suit-clad driver exits the vehicle to assist with my stuff. I forgo his helping hand, placing my shit in the trunk myself. There's only a medium-sized suitcase and a carry-on bag inside. Color me surprised. At least Emma's sensible. I won't deny I was expecting multiple bags from her.

She's already waiting for me inside the car, messing with her phone when I slide in.

"Weather's nice in Ireland this weekend," she ways without lifting her head.

I figure this is the time to lay down the ground rules. "Listen, Emma. As much as I admire your determination, you really have to start listening to what I say."

Her eyebrows are furrowed when she turns to me. "Wait? Are you mad that I came to pick you up? I was just being nice, Rori."

I shift on the seat so I can better look at her. I don't miss when she drops her gaze to my chest. It's not the first time I've caught her staring at me like that. She made it no secret that she was attracted to me before, but she's hasn't yet recovered the memories from that night she came on to me. My guess is that she won't try to seduce me again, not when she's on a mission to find her soul mate.

"I don't need to be pampered," I say. "Understand that when I say no to you, I'm not issuing a challenge."

Her eyes narrow to slits. "Fine. Have it your way. I'll be a downright bitch to you, then. I'm really good at it too."

And don't I know it. I still remember what she said to me before she closed the door in my face. The worst part is that she may be right. I can totally see myself on my knees, begging.

"Does everything have to be extremes with you? How about just regular Emma?"

She whips her face to mine so fast, I almost flinch away. "What's that supposed to mean?"

Shit, I must've touched a sore subject. Nothing I say now is going to save me. "Never mind."

Her green eyes spark with anger before her lips turn into a pout. Without another word, she turns to the window, crossing her arms.

Damn it. Maybe this was a huge mistake. But it's too late to back down from my offer now. I wish I could read minds, because I'm at complete loss about what I said that triggered her like that.

I thought I had her figured out when she walked into my pub, but the more time I spend with her, the more I realize how wrong I was.

***

EMMA

"REGULAR EMMA." WHAT THE HELL DOES HE MEAN BY THAT? I'M NOT an over-the-top person, am I?

I don't say another word to the guy during the car ride. I don't want to so much as glance in his direction—more so because I can't stop ogling him, but that's another story. Why does he have to be infuriating and sexy in equal measures?

In the airport, I walk ahead. I'm flying business class, so my line to drop off luggage is shorter than his. Out of spite, I don't tell him that I upgraded his ticket to business class too. Let him wait longer. I also don't want to hear his complaints when he learns I went against his wishes again.

As a matter of fact, I'm regretting my decision already. The prospect of being stuck next to him for the next ten hours is getting less appealing by the minute.

I spare him one brief glance before I head for security. He looks up, his face an unreadable mask. I catch my breath, despite my annoyance. God, the man is beautiful. He has his hair bound again in a bun, and I can't decide if I like him better like that or with it loose. Warmth unfurls in my belly and my heart begins to pound faster. I really have to stop having these reactions around the guy.

With a clench of the jaw, I turn away, remembering I'm supposed to be pissed at him.

I don't see Rori in the security line, and I wonder how mad he is at me. Surely he knows about his upgrade by now. He doesn't come to the business class lounge—which isn't a surprise—so my guess is he's pissed. When they announce my flight is ready for boarding, I put on my resting bitch face as I head toward the gate. I spot him right away, sitting next to an elderly couple, and he's laughing. *What the hell!* And here I was expecting to find him brooding. But no, he's engaged in an animated conversation with those strangers. I feel like a fool for bothering to put up a show of indifference for him. He's clearly winning.

As predicted, Rori doesn't join me in the priority line to board. This time, I manage not to look in his direction, pretending I don't know him. My resting bitch face is real now as I greet the stewardess with a tight smile.

Rori doesn't show up until much later, and my guess is he was one of the last passengers to board. The sugary tone with which the stewardess addresses him is what clues me in to his arrival. I keep staring out the window, not even glancing at him when he sits next to me. I only move when the stewardess offers me a glass of Prosecco. I wasn't planning to start drinking so soon, but fuck if I don't need alcohol right now.

Rori keeps staring ahead, a perfect statue, as I reach across him to get my drink.

"Anything for you, sir?" the stewardess asks him.

"No, I'm good for now. Thank you."

I'm halfway through my drink when he finally talks to me. "What other surprises do you have waiting for me?"

"I don't know what you're talking about." I take a sip of my drink.

"Drop the act, Emma. Do you have us booked in the most expensive hotel in Dublin too?"

I had every intention to not look at the guy for the entire duration of our flight, but it's kind of hard to glare at someone without looking at them. "No. I didn't book anything. You said you had the hotel covered. I trust you *did* book rooms for us."

He turns to me, scowling. "Yes, Emma, I took care of that. I'm perfectly capable of making travel arrangements and going from A to B without help."

"I never said you weren't. Lighten up, will you? It's just a ticket upgrade, big freaking deal."

"It is a big deal since I said I didn't want it."

"Fine! You're more than welcome to give up your seat and go sit in the tuna can area."

I look out the window again, fury making my blood pump faster.

"Believe me, I tried," he grumbles.

His words sting, and I feel stupid for letting Rori get to me like that. Why do I care if he likes me or appreciates my thoughtful gestures anyway? I'm not trying to seduce him; he's just a guide after all, one I probably don't need.

I attempt to ignore his presence next to mine, something

easier said than done. It's an impossible task, not only because of the bulk of his frame but because the guy seems to radiate heat. I'm like a moth attracted to his flame. It's also irritating as hell to hear the stewardess flirt shamelessly with him.

To compensate, I keep drinking, glad the woman is too busy paying attention to Rori to keep count of my alcohol intake. They usually don't curb passengers in business class, but I know I'm pushing the limits. My bladder agrees.

I don't have to bother Rori to reach the aisle since there's ample room in front of our seats for me to walk out, but I do sense his eyes follow me when I cross in front of him.

In the restroom, I take my time fixing my appearance because I'm a fucking silly woman. I wipe off the mascara smudge under my eyes and pinch my cheeks to get some color back in. I forgot how the cabin's dry air turns everyone into ghosts.

We hit a patch of turbulence just as I'm heading back to my seat, and I end up falling onto Rori's lap.

"Sorry," I say, my cheeks now in flames.

"No problem."

Is it my imagination, or are Rori's hands lingering on my back longer than necessary? I finally get to my seat and buckle up. The shaking has increased, and the seat belt sign is on. A sudden drop makes me jump out of my skin, and my stomach bottoms out. I may have let out a little scream. I feel Rori's stare, but I'm too busy fighting the panic that's spreading through my chest. I was never afraid to fly before, but the noise and the shaking seem to have triggered memories that I've tried so hard to suppress.

Damn it, I wish I hadn't drunk so much. I won't be able to take my medication now—which I hate doing anyway.

This is not the metro, Emma. Get a grip on yourself.

Rori covers my hand with his, and that's when I notice I was gripping the armrest with all my strength.

"Relax, Emma. It's only air."

I look at him, breathing through my nose, struggling with my emotions. I know it's only air, but I can't get my brain to stop sending panic signals to my body.

"Focus on your breathing. Take a deep breath and exhale slowly." He demonstrates, and I copy him.

Little by little, my heart rate returns to normal and the pressure in my chest lessens. It helps that the plane has moved out of the turbulence patch.

Without the panic, I finally notice Rori is making lazy circles over my hand with the tip of his thumb. The awareness causes goose bumps to break out on my skin, and my breathing hitches for entirely different reasons.

My lips open slightly as I stare at his mouth, craving a taste.

"Emma?"

"Yeah?" I ask in a daze.

"Are you feeling better?"

I look into his warm hazel eyes and find worry there, mixed with something else. I would guess desire, but I can't trust my instincts right now.

"Yes, thank you."

I pull my hand from under his because the contact is making it harder for me to concentrate. I'm not going to Ireland to fall into bed with Rori, as much as my body wants to.

8

———

EMMA

March 2017, Dublin

LIGHT SHAKING ON MY SHOULDER TRIES TO DISTURB MY PEACE. I curl into a tighter ball, pulling the blanket over my head. Sleeping is too good, and whatever it is they want, it's not worth waking up to find out. The fabric is pushed off my face and someone with facial hair and warm, minty breath whispers in my ear.

"Wakey, wakey."

Awareness hits me all at once and I jump in my seat with a start. The sound of a male chuckle nearby finishes waking me up for good.

"What happened? What time is it?" I rub my eyes, then pull the window slide up. Bright sunlight comes through the glass, making me wince. I block it again and turn to Rori, who's watching me with a smirk on his lips.

"What are you looking at?" I ask.

"You. I had no idea you were such a heavy sleeper."

I feel my cheeks getting warm. Embarrassed, I lean forward

to grab the toiletries pouch from my bag. "I'm usually not. It was the booze."

"Figures. You were down for the count pretty quickly last night, even missed dinner."

A terrible thought occurs to me. "I didn't snore, did I?"

When Rori doesn't answer right away, I risk a glance in his direction. He's watching me, still sporting that cat-that-ate-the-canary grin and a glint of amusement in his eyes. I straighten up in my seat, clutching the pouch to my chest. "I did?"

Finally, he shakes his head. "No, Emma. You didn't."

I exhale loudly in relief. How mortifying it would've been if I'd snored—not that I should care what Rori thinks. Although, I should probably go freshen up. God knows what I look like right now. If I'm to judge by the taste of ashes in my mouth, it's a safe bet that I look like death. The opposite of Rori, who seems to have just sprung out of a fashion magazine.

Heat rushes to my face. *He whispered in my ear. Why would he do such a thing?*

My mortification increases tenfold when I catch my reflection in the mirror. *Oh my God.* My mascara has run down, creating a lovely raccoon effect underneath my eyes—which are bloodshot, by the way, thanks to me sleeping with my contacts in. The right side of my hair is so tangled it resembles a bird's nest. There's also a path of dried drool starting at the corner of my mouth.

Fuck me.

I wash my face, wishing it would also wash away Rori's memory of my pitiful sight. Getting rid of the knots in my hair proves more difficult. I had forgotten how easily it tangles when it's blonder. I lose a big chunk of it in the process.

Knowing I won't be able to wear new contacts for the next several hours, I go heavy on the eyeliner and mascara. It's the only way to look good wearing glasses. I brush my teeth twice, but still can't get rid of the foul taste in my mouth. Maybe once

I eat breakfast it'll fade, but I'll be popping mints left and right today.

Once my face is taken care off, I glance at my top. It's a little wrinkled from sleeping in it, but since I forgot to bring a change of clothing with me, it'll have to do.

Breakfast has already been served when I return to my seat. I see a tray waiting for me. The only thing I don't see is how I'm gonna get to my seat now. Business class has ample leg room, but not so much when the folded trays are down. Without skipping a beat, Rori springs to his feet, with both my breakfast and his in hand. If I attempted that move, I would've ended up spilling everything onto the floor.

I mumble a thank-you as I slide into my seat, my stomach grumbling at the prospect of food. I sense Rori's stare as he sits back down, but I refuse to acknowledge him.

"I didn't know you wear glasses."

"There's a lot you don't know about me." I shove a piece of bread into my mouth.

"True. They suit you."

I give him a droll look. "No, they don't. They make me look like a nerd."

"What's wrong with that?" The corners of his lips twitch up.

"I don't know if you're being serious or if you're mocking me."

He switches his attention back to his tray and says, "Maybe after this trip you'll be able to tell."

"Right. Anyway, I forgot to ask you. Did you ask your folks about the Kellys you thought they knew?"

"No."

"Why not? You said you would."

Rori puts his knife down with a groan and looks at me. "Because they would want to know why I was looking for a Declan Kelly, and I didn't want to talk about the specifics of our deal over the phone. Don't worry. I'll ask them in person."

"I *am* worried. I've found no trace of Declan anywhere I looked. Your parents could've already started making inquiries. We don't have a lot of time, you know?"

"I know. Again, don't worry. We'll have enough time. Kinsale is a village. Somebody is bound to know your guy."

I clench my jaw as I catch a hint of mockery in Rori's tone. He doesn't need to say it out loud, but I know he thinks what I'm doing is nuts. And perhaps it *is* crazy, but I made a promise to Dad and I intend to keep it. I saw it as a sign that Rori was from the same hometown as Declan and that he had a trip planned already. The only hitch in the plan was Dad's recovery. I wouldn't be able to go anywhere if he was still in the hospital, but the man is as strong as a bull. He was released a week after his heart attack.

Our flight lands in the next hour, and despite traveling business class, I can't help the need to stretch my body. I'm keen to leave this metal box and explore Dublin again. I hope Rori proves to be a great guide.

As we walk through the airport, I notice the glances Rori gets from women and sometimes even men. I get my own share of attention as well, but it's mostly chicks throwing an envious glace my way. The hint of annoyance simmers below my skin. I'm nothing to the guy, but I can't imagine what it would be like if I were his girlfriend. For starters, I'd have to amp up my hair care so I could match his glorious mane. And I'd probably have to take up some type of martial arts to keep the skanks away from him. The thought is so ludicrous it makes me chuckle.

"What's so funny?" he asks.

"Nothing."

I sense Rori staring at me, so I turn to him. Shit, big mistake. I don't know what's different about his gaze today, but the intensity in his hazel eyes robs me of breath.

I couldn't have found a guide who I wasn't attracted to, could I?

Grinding my teeth, I break the connection and vow to avoid

making eye contact with the man. Our luggage takes forever to come through the carousel, and the silence stretching between us becomes a tangible thing. I begin to shift my weight from foot to foot in a fidgety motion, hating that he's making me this uncomfortable. I'm usually pretty chill in most awkward situations; what is it about Rori that makes me so unraveled?

He offers to help me with my luggage, but I want to prove that I'm not a pampered rich girl. Somehow, his earlier erroneous perception of me is still chafing my ego.

We emerge from the arrivals exit walking side by side, and our appearance causes a ruckus in the crowd. A group of three burly men shouts Rori's name, and then they proceed to tackle him in an overly enthusiastic manner. They don't seem to notice me, so I move to the side to avoid getting swept under the melee and watch this unexpected outcome unfold. When I can finally see Rori's face, I note both surprise and dismay.

"Bloody hell, lad. How come we have to hear from your sister that you were coming to Dublin?" one of Rori's friends asks.

The guy has a mohawk and long hipster beard, but he's wearing a perfectly tailored suit, which is an odd contrast. He has symbols tattooed on each finger, and when he moves his arm, I catch sight of an expensive-looking watch. The fact that I noticed all that within seconds is probably my upbringing showing. When you grow up surrounded by the wealthiest and most famous people in the world, you learn to analyze a person's appearance pretty quickly. It's not a matter of being shallow—it's survival.

"It was a last-minute thing," Rori says.

"I call horse-shit, but it's okay. You'll compensate for it tonight by picking up the tab." He throws an arm around Rori's shoulder.

The tallest of Rori's friends, shorter only in comparison to him, turns my way. I have to do a double take because he's pretty much Jesse Williams's doppelganger, down to the gorgeous green eyes and easy smile.

"Oh, hello there," he says. "I'm Miles, and you are?"

"Emma." I extend my hand. "Nice to meet you, Miles."

We shake hands and Miles turns to Rori. "You're full of secrets, Rori."

The third friend, a stocky guy with a mop of curly brown hair, watches me with appreciation shining in his eyes. *Seriously, dude? Despite my best attempt to fix my appearance, I still look like hell, and I have nerdy glasses on.*

"You always get the good ones, Rori," he says.

I open my mouth to clarify that Rori and I are not together when, to my surprise, Rori throws an arm around my shoulder and pulls me close. "I sure do." He kisses the top of my head, making a million questions pop up in my brain, the first being *What the hell is going on here?*

Not knowing the reason why Rori decided to lie to his friends, I play along with the charade, but he'd better have a pretty good explanation for it. I didn't sign up to pretend to be his girlfriend.

"All right, let's get going," mohawk guy says.

"Where are we going exactly?" Rori asks, suspicion lacing his words.

Miles chuckles. "Don't worry. We're just dropping you off at the hotel. I'm sure you want to rest."

"I'm not sure if there will be a lot of resting," the stocky friend laughs.

"For fuck's sake. Take your mind out of the gutter, Dimitri," Rori grumbles.

I'm usually way more social, but I'm feeling out of my depth thanks to Rori's deception, so I bite my tongue and observe the interaction between him and his friends. But I can't wait to grill him later.

Mohawk guy drives us in his fully equipped beemer SUV. I

learn his name is Lewis McGregor and he's a very successful entrepreneur, the owner of a hipster burger chain of restaurants. Miles and Dimitri take off in their separate cars, saying they'll see us later tonight.

To keep Lewis from asking any questions about my fake relationship with Rori, I'm the one who gives him the third-degree. He seems happy to talk about himself and only asks me what I do for a living. That immediately veers the conversation to business, and before I know it, we arrive at our hotel.

"What's the plan?" Rori asks.

"Well, I figured I'd let you guys rest, and I'll be back to you pick you up around four. Are you planning to do any sight-seeing?"

Rori turns in his seat to look at me. "It's up to what Emma wants to do."

I shrug. "It doesn't matter to me. I've been to Dublin before."

With a nod, Rori turns back to his friend. "We'll be ready by four."

Lewis is double-parked in front of the hotel, so he only helps take the luggage out of the truck and doesn't linger.

Finally alone with Rori, I open my mouth to grill him, but he speaks before I can.

"Sorry about that. I didn't expect an ambush."

"Why did you lie to your friends about the status of our relationship?"

He pauses and rubs his face. "Dimitri is a notorious manwhore. If I hadn't told him we were together, he would pester you the entire time."

I cross my arms in front of my chest. "That's the reason you lied? What, you don't think I can fend off the likes of Dimitri?"

Rori shakes his head and frowns at me. "Trust me, Emma. I did you a favor."

"How thoughtful of you."

I turn on my heels and march inside the hotel. I'm pissed that Rori would treat me in such a condescending way. Do I look like I need help dealing with assholes?

I'm in a foul mood when I approach the reception desk. Rori follows me but is wise enough to leave some distance between us. The guy finds our reservation, but he tells me only one room is ready for check-in.

"You can take that one," Rori says.

"Gee, thanks."

"Emma, don't be like that."

Not wanting to air dirty laundry in front of strangers, I ignore Rori's comment. I could've offered to store his stuff in my room, but instead I grab my keycard and leave him in the lobby without a word.

9

———

RORI

I COULDN'T REST DURING THE DAY TO SAVE TO MY LIFE; NOT EVEN the walk through the neighborhood helped me relax. My mind was too busy running through the events of the last twenty-four hours.

I still don't have an explanation to why I lied to my friends about Emma. Dimitri can be obnoxious when it comes to women, but it didn't warrant my deception.

I rub my face, struggling with the obvious realization that I've developed an unhealthy attachment to the woman, despite my vow to stay away. First, the offer to help her track another guy, and now this. I need to get my head straight if I'm to survive the week in Kinsale.

I haven't heard from her the entire day, but Lewis will be here soon, so I'd better straighten things out with her before-hand. As fate would have it, Emma is in the room next to mine. It's the interconnected type, so I press my ear against the door and hear the sound of muffled music. She doesn't know I'm in the room next to hers, so I walk outside to knock on her hallway door.

She doesn't answer right away, so I knock harder. "Emma, I know you're in there. Can we talk?"

The music cuts off suddenly, and a second later the door swings open, revealing a furious and stunning Emma. I have to lock my jaw tight to avoid it dropping to the floor. She's wearing a long-sleeve wrap dress with a very revealing neckline, her lacy bra peeking from it. I knew she had nice boobs, but fuck me, I can't help trying to imagine what they look like underneath her clothes. Her skirt is flowy, but it's also very short. I was planning to tell the guys I'd lied about Emma being my girlfriend, but I'm having second thoughts. If Dimitri learns she's available, he'll be all over her like a hobo on a hotdog.

"What do you want?" she asks.

"May I come in?"

"If you must." She opens the door wider and walks back inside.

I'm not going to look at her ass. I'm not going to loo—damn it. Failed. I don't see a single panty line. Oh man, I hope she's not going commando. I can't remember what I wanted to talk about anymore. All my blood has flooded down to my crotch, leaving my brain useless.

She turns, still glaring, and crosses her arms. Her boobs are pushed up in the process, making my mouth even drier.

"Are you going to spill it on your own, or do I need to tip you over?" she asks.

I shake my head, seeing if I can kick-start my brain. God, why am I behaving like a stupid, hormonal teenager?

"Rori?"

"Uh, right. I want to apologize for what I said earlier. I shouldn't have lied to the guys."

"No, you shouldn't have." She turns to the desk behind her, diverting her attention to the pile of sparkling accessories on it. She picks up a dangling earring, inspecting it for a second before discarding it and selecting another one.

"I'll tell them the truth tonight," I continue.

"Don't bother."

I narrow my eyes at her, even though she can't see my reaction. "Now I'm confused."

She turns to me and raises an eyebrow, her emerald green eyes sparkling with mischief. "I've decided to use your lie to make you suffer."

Clenching my jaw, I take a step closer. "Is that so? I can't possibly imagine how you'll accomplish that."

"Oh, you'll have to wait and see." Her lips curl into a sassy grin, and of course, my gaze immediately zeroes in on them. She has no idea how her open challenge is making my blood pump faster, how I want to ignore all the warning in my head and kiss her until her legs turn to mush.

I take a step back before I give in to the urge, already knowing it's futile to fight. Whatever happens during this trip, it will not end well for me.

Emma

I have no idea how I'm going to make Rori pay, but his reaction gives me a thrill I haven't felt in days. I'm playing a dangerous game here. This cruel teasing is a trademark move on my part when I want to score some booty. The only problem is Rori and any other guy are off-limits. I need to keep my focus on the prize.

Lewis picks us up at four o'clock sharp, and we head to a local pub for happy hour. Since it's Saturday, the place is already fairly busy, but Lewis knows the bartender and we score a table which is apparently reserved for regulars. Miles and Dimitri are already there. I get appreciative glances from both men when I remove my jacket, Dimitri going as far as whistling loudly, which earns him a backhand slap from Miles.

"Quit being such a stook," Miles says, then turns to us. "I hope you two are rested, because tonight will be hatched."

"Oh, I can't wait," Rori replies with a roll of his eyes.

"So, Em—may I call you Em?" Dimitri leans forward.

"Sure." I shrug.

"What possessed you to start dating this wanker here?" Dimitri points at Rori, who sits straighter in his chair.

I look at him with a smirk. "Well, a friend of mine used to play at his pub. Rori was pretty smitten the first time he saw me, even though I was absolutely not interested."

Rori lips turn into a thin, flat line as he stares at me through slits. However, there's a slight upward twitch of his lips, which tells me he's not completely displeased with my story. I need to up my game. *I am going to make you suffer, Rori.*

"I'm not surprised. You're a ten, while Rori here is a seven at best," Dimitri says with a laugh. "No offense, mate."

A seven? Is he kidding? Rori is a fucking eleven.

"So, what made you change your mind?" Lewis raises his arm to call the attention of a waiter.

"Restless pursuing. Stalking territory, really."

"Stalking, huh?" Rori raises an eyebrow, smirking at me now. *Why is he amused? I'm not doing this right.*

"Yeah, that sounds like Rori all right." Miles chuckles.

"Shut your face." Rori throws a cardboard coaster at his friend.

"Wait." My hand goes up. "What do you mean that sounds like Rori? Did he ever pull that stunt with another girl?" I look at each of his friends, noticing the amusement quickly vanish from their faces.

"Er, you didn't tell her about—"

"Let's just drop it." Rori's frown is real, and the sudden

change in his attitude gives me a whiplash. I wanted to push his buttons, but I sense I've veered into heavily mined terrain.

If I were his real girlfriend, I'd be pretty upset about his attitude. But I'm not, and I'm not going to ruin our evening just for the sake of pretenses.

I wave dismissively. "It doesn't matter. He was pretty persistent and ended up winning me over. The rest is history." I squeeze his thigh and place a soft kiss on his cheek. He tenses a bit, but then he grants me a tight smile.

"Drinks? My treat," I say.

"No, no. We can't have a lass paying for our drinks. That would make us no better than pigs."

Lewis places an order of pints, but I'm actually craving something stronger. I was never a fan of beer. I excuse myself to look for a restroom, but what I really want is to give Rori some space. There's something about his past that he clearly doesn't wish his friends to disclose to me. Having a huge secret of my own, I don't begrudge him that.

On the way back from the restroom, I decide to order a round of shots, because in my world, women can pay for drinks too.

When I return, I find Rori laughing with his friends, the tension from before obviously gone.

"I come bearing goods," I say with tray in hand.

"Blimey, woman. What did we say about not buying us drinks?" Lewis says.

"Oh, Emma doesn't know the meaning of the word no," Rori adds, giving me a loaded look.

"I certainly don't. To me, it only means we're open to negotiations."

"That's right. You have to be persistent if you want to achieve anything in life. If I had accepted the first no thrown my way, I'd probably still be cleaning toilets in a shitty restaurant." Lewis grabs his shot glass and salutes me with it.

"For fuck's sake, you're not going to start talking business, are you?" Miles whines.

Lewis elbows his friend's arm and laughs.

"How long have you guys known each other?" I ask.

"Since we were wee lads. Seven or eight years old?" Rori replies.

Dimitri nods. "That sounds about right."

"We were in a football club together. You know, what you call soccer." Rori looks at me.

"Yeah, I know what you mean."

"Our boy here was the star of the team, the best forward that little small town had ever seen." Lewis claps Rori's shoulder.

"Really? I didn't know that." I watch Rori intently. His face is closed off again.

"Fuck, Rori. How long have you been dating this girl? She knows nothing," Dimitri asks.

Rori shifts in his chair and takes a long sip of his beer. I don't know if he's mad or embarrassed, but he's clearly not having a good time. I feel bad now even though I did nothing wrong.

"Not long, really. Just over a month," I say.

"And he's already bringing you to meet his family?" Dimitri whistles. "Boy, either he truly loves you or he wants to scare you away."

Heat rushes to my cheeks and my heart skips a beat. This is ridiculous. I barely tolerate the guy, and I know not to confuse lust with love. I pick up my shot glass and drink the tequila in one gulp.

"Are we eating here, or should we go someplace else?" Miles asks.

"How about I treat you guys to the best burgers in town?" Lewis smiles.

"Free dinner at the Hipster Burger? I'm in." Dimitri rubs his hands together.

We finish our drinks and head out. Lewis's restaurant isn't far from the pub, so we walk. Rori and I fall behind while his friends goof around ahead. Boys will always be boys no matter how old they are.

Rori laces his arm with mine, and it sends shivers up my spine.

He's only keeping up the pretense, Emma. Chill out.

"What was Dimitri going to say back there when you cut him off?" I ask, even though it's none of my business.

"Nothing. Don't worry about it."

"I suppose if we're going to pretend we're a couple for the evening, we should know some basics about each other."

"Very well. I have two sisters. Keira, the one getting married, is two years older than me, and—"

"Hold up. I just realized I don't know your age."

"I'm twenty-seven. My birthday is November 5^(th)."

"I'm twenty—"

"Two," Rori finishes my sentence. "I know."

"How?"

"I, uh... Saylor told me."

"Why?" I turn to him, suspicion lacing my words.

"I can't remember."

Bullcrap. What's he keeping from me now?

"Anyway," he continues, "my youngest sister is Lizzy. She's sixteen and a brat. Don't take it personally if she's not super-friendly to you at first. Keira's fiancé is a French guy named Claude, but everyone calls him by his last name, Clemmot. They were high school sweethearts. Expect plenty of jokes about that. The family's been pestering Keira for ages about her long-ass relationship with the guy. My parents are Anne and Gerard, and they've been married for thirty-five years. They own a farm bed-and-breakfast. We're staying there, by the way. I couldn't get out of it."

My head is spinning with the overload of information.

"That's a lot of names to remember. I'm much easier. It's just me and Dad. My mother passed away when I was two, and I have no memories of her. Dad is a big-shot divorce lawyer in LA, and his clients are mostly celebrities."

"I'm sorry about your mum. Your father never remarried?"

I snort. "Yes, and way too many times, if you ask me. I stopped counting after the third wife."

"We couldn't have come from more different backgrounds," Rori says with a tone of surprise, as if he just came to that realization.

"Is that a problem? I mean, hypothetically, if we were a real couple."

Rori stops and turns to me. He locks his gaze with mine, and the air is sucked out of my lungs. It feels like I'm being swept off my feet. If this was another time, I would've kissed him.

"If we were a real couple, it wouldn't matter at all." He raises his hand to touch my hair but stops in the last second.

Damn it. I wanted to know what his caress would feel like.

"Hey, you guys coming or what?" Lewis yells at us from farther ahead.

"Coming," Rori replies, still looking into my eyes. I should look away, I should stop whatever's happening here, but I can't.

Hell and damn. I'm counting on him to be the strong one. If he succumbs to the crazy sexual tension between us, I don't think I'll be strong enough to walk away.

10

RORI

My jaw is hanging open as I stare at Emma polishing off the biggest cheeseburger Lewis has on the menu. The thing is massive, and even I had trouble eating the whole thing. My friends have equally perplexed expressions on their faces.

"How does she fit all that in?" Dimitri whispers to himself.

"She even ate all the fries," Miles adds.

Only after Emma shoves the last bite of her greasy meal in does she notice the attention. She cleans her face with a napkin and asks after swallowing her food, "What? Do I have ketchup on my face?"

"I can't believe you ate the whole thing," Lewis says, mesmerized.

"This little thing?" She pshaws with her hand. "It was nothing."

"All the girls I dated in the past only ordered salads." Miles rests his chin on his closed fist and watches Emma with a love-struck gleam in his eyes. I feel the urge to hit him upside the head. That's my girlfriend he's ogling.

Your fake girlfriend, Rori. Don't forget that.

Emma twists her face into a grimace, then takes a big sip of her soda. "Yeah, I'm not one of those chicks who tries to impress guys by not eating. I like food too much."

"Man, forget Rori. Marry me?" Dimitri jokes, but I know if it weren't for my fake relationship with Emma, he'd be dead serious—not about the marriage proposal, but what comes before the wedding, aka the fucking part.

Emma pretends to scrutinize me by narrowing her eyes and wrinkling her nose. She looks too fucking cute doing that, and I want to pull her closer and... ah hell, do what? Kiss her? I can't go there. I was close enough to doing so earlier.

She looks at Dimitri for a brief moment before shaking her head and scooching closer to me in the booth. "Nah, I think I'll keep my Tarzan."

"Stop with the mushy stuff. You're gonna make me sick." Miles sticks his tongue out and pretends he's on the verge of throwing up.

"Tarzan?" I ask.

She smiles from ear to ear, making her eyes sparkle with an emotion I can't decipher, but I want to. "The hair." She runs her finger over my head, and a zing of pleasure races down my spine "The beard." She glides her hand down my face until she's cupping my jaw. "You're a better Tarzan than Alex Skarsgård ever was."

My heart is pounding, and I swear if my friends weren't here, I'd be fucking her mouth with my tongue already. I don't know when the change happened, but my mind has already forgotten the night she got so out of control that she can't remember. Our bodies are closer than they were before, our arms and legs touching. Maybe it's all innocent, but my body hasn't gotten the memo. On the contrary, it's reacting as if we're in an incendiary act of foreplay. My cock is rock-hard, straining against my jeans. I'll need a cold shower when I get back to the hotel.

"Okay, where to next?" Dimitri asks, breaking the spell between Emma and me.

As if in a trance, I turn to my friends. "What do you have in mind?"

"Let's go to Willies & Nillies. They have a great house beer and pool tables."

"Right. It has nothing to do with the hot women who like to hang out there," Lewis says with a knowing smile.

"Hey, nothing wrong with that. Since I have zero chance with Emma, I have to find other options. Little Dimka is lonely."

"Oh my God, did you just refer to your dick?" Emma laughs.

"Of course. All guys do that." Dimitri leans back, frowning as if offended.

"I don't." Lewis takes a large sip of his beer while looking at Emma from the corner of his eye.

Emma turns to me. "Rori?"

I raise both hands. "I plead the fifth."

She hits my chest with the back of her hand. "Shut up. You do it too? What do you call it?"

"Wait, you don't know?" Miles asks.

Without missing a beat, Emma throws a glance his way. "Obviously not. We've only been dating for a month."

I need to stop this conversation pronto. Emma talking about my dick is not helping me get my raging erection down one bit. "If we're going to another place, let's get going. The jetlag is starting to get to me."

"We gotta drive. I think if we squeeze a little, you can all fit in my car." Lewis stands, grabbing his jacket in the process.

Since we're dining with the boss, we head out without bothering with the bill. It's a five-minute walk back to where Lewis parked his car, and the fresh night air helps clear my head a little. My erection is still there, though. Jesus, when was the last time I woman got me so horny like that?

Things don't get any easier for me when we hop into the car. Emma insists on sitting in the middle since she's the shortest, and Dimitri, the asshole he is, makes no attempt to avoid rubbing his legs against hers. I pull her closer to me in an idiotic protective gesture, even though she's not mine.

In an unbelievable struck of good luck, Lewis finds a parking spot right in front of the popular bar in the basement of an old church. I place a hand on Emma's lower back, but she freezes on the sidewalk while my friends disappear down the stairs.

"What's wrong?"

"I-I can't go in there."

"The bar? Why not?"

When she doesn't answer right away, I move in front of her and rest my hands on her upper arms. "Emma, talk to me."

She raises her gaze to mine. There's fear there, and I'm at a complete loss as to what to do. She was fine a minute ago.

"I can't be in underground places. It triggers... this."

"A panic attack?"

She nods.

"We don't need to go in there. I'll tell the guys. They'll understand."

"No, you haven't seen them in ages. I don't want to be a burden. I'll just get a cab back to the hotel."

"No, that's out of the question." I pull my phone from my jacket pocket, ready to text Lewis, when Emma covers my hand with hers.

"Don't do it. Maybe if you help me, I can manage. This isn't the subway. It's just a bar, right?"

"Em, it's really okay if we don't go in there."

"You called me Em." She laughs nervously. "I must be really freaking you out."

God, I didn't realize the slip. But I'm not going to lie and say I'm not worried. Something bad happened to Emma in an underground place, and she's still suffering from PSTD. That much is clear to me. Maybe it's related to her scar.

"Just focus on your breathing like you did in the airplane during the turbulence. Fill your lungs and exhale slowly."

She does as I tell her while I rub her arms up and down. She maintains eye contact with me through the whole exercise, and I wish I could do more to help. It takes a minute or so for her shaking to subside.

"Are you feeling better?" I ask.

"A little." She glances behind me, no doubt eyeing the stars going down. I'm about to offer that we go back to the hotel again when she continues. "Could you hold my hand?"

"Of course." I lace our hands together and take a step toward the stairs. She follows me, but right before I take the first step down, I turn to her. "If you don't feel comfortable inside, just say the word and we'll leave, okay?"

"Deal. Thank you, Rori."

Emma's confident personality is one of the things that attracts me to her, but seeing her so terrified shifts something inside of me. There's a sudden need to protect her that I'm powerless to stop. I didn't expect to feel anything like this for any woman.

The bar is almost full to the capacity, and it doesn't take me long to see why my friends didn't come to see what the holdup was. Dimitri's scored a pool table and is showing off to some girls. Miles and Lewis are each equally occupied with women of their own.

"Wow. Your friends don't waste time."

"Nope."

"You must've been quite the heartbreakers when you were young."

I chuckle. "Not quite. Are you sure you're good?" She still looks pale, but at least the panic's gone from her eyes.

"Yeah. So far so good." She stretches her neck and looks around. "Do you know where the restrooms are?"

I point to the end of the bar where the sign says 'Restrooms.'

"Thanks. I'll be right back." She takes a step forward, but I'm still holding her hand and I don't let go. I squeeze it a little instead.

"What would you like to drink?"

"Anything but beer. Surprise me." She gives me a half smile and I swear to God, my heart does a little somersault.

What the actual fuck. I'm a grown man. I shouldn't be reacting like a teenager.

I brace the crowd and head for the bar. I'm glad I'm taller than most, so it's easier for me to make eye contact with the bartender without obstruction. It takes me a minute to get his attention though—it's a madhouse in here. I figure it's easier to leave the tab open, and I've just handed the guy my credit card when Lewis materializes next to me.

"Hey, want something to drink?" I ask.

"No, I'm good. I come bearing bad news."

Lewis ominous tone makes me immediately think about Emma. *Did something happen to her while I was busy getting the drinks?*

"Is it Emma?"

"No, mate, it's not about Emma. Well, it could be. I wanted to warn you that Alannah is here."

"What?" I feel the blood drain from my face. I haven't seen her since I left Ireland for good, and my friends know not to bring her name up. "I didn't know she was in Dublin."

"Yeah, it's my fault. I mentioned by accident that you were coming into town. She must've seen my update that we were heading here and decided to surprise you."

Jesus, why must Lewis be such a social media whore?

"I don't know what for." I drink the shot of whiskey I

ordered, feeling the need to drown my irritation with alcohol. I guess time hasn't eased the resentment I have for the woman I thought was the one.

I drink the shot meant for Emma as well and order two more before following Lewis to the pool table area. I spot Alannah right away. She still wears her pitch-black hair long and straight. Her face is partially hidden by a baseball cap, but the gold hoop earrings are clearly visible. Even her style hasn't changed.

She turns to me and her caked face breaks into a smile. I used to melt every time she looked at me like that, but right now it just rubs me the wrong way.

"Rori. Oh my God. You're a sight for sore eyes." She engulfs me into a tight hug, a gesture I don't reciprocate.

Noticing my lack of reaction, she steps back, her smile wilted. "It's good to see you," she adds.

"Hi, Alannah." I move away since she doesn't seem inclined to get out of my personal space.

Her face morphs into an expression of hurt. "Wow. That's all I get after everything we've been through?"

My friends become scarce, and I don't blame them. Two seconds in her presence and this shit is already awkward.

"I'm not sure what you expect from me. I haven't contacted you in nine years despite your several attempts to keep in touch. If that isn't clue enough, I don't know what is."

Her brown eyes fill with tears, a move she used to pull all the time when we were dating. It took me months after we broke up to realize how much she manipulated me. I was such a fool.

"You don't know how much I've regretted my decision, Rori. We were young, and you were so broken. I didn't know what to do."

"Please, let's not do this. It's been almost a decade. I don't see why we have to talk about the past. I've moved on, and I sure hope you have too."

She takes a step closer and touches my chest. "What if I told you I haven't moved on?"

"I'd say it's too fucking bad," Emma says in a tone that leaves no room for interpretation. She's pissed.

11

EMMA

I THROW COLD WATER ON MY CHEEKS EVEN THOUGH I'M RISKING ruining my makeup. I didn't expect to be faced with a situation that would trigger a panic attack. How was I supposed to know we would come to bar in a basement? The idea of being trapped underground again makes my lungs close off.

I've never been able to conquer the fear until Rori entered the picture. I don't know if it was his steadfast presence, the determination in his gaze, or his reassuring touch that did the trick. It could've been his voice—strong and soothing at the same time—that managed to bridge the irrational cloud of paralyzing fear. Now I'm left with no choice but to tell him about my past. I don't want him thinking I'm a basket case.

My face is pale, so I apply a fresh coat of lipstick to add some color. My eye makeup is holding strong, so I leave it alone. With a deep breath and one final glance at my reflection, I venture back into the busy bar.

I have to fight my way back to the main room. It seems the crowd has doubled in the two minutes I was gone, or maybe I was so out of it, I didn't notice the place was this busy. I stretch my neck, searching for Rori.

First I look in the bar's direction, since he said he would get us drinks. When I don't find him, I expand my search perimeter, finding him not too far from where I stand, by the pool tables. He's talking with a woman, and his friends are nowhere to be seen. I pinch my lips and make a beeline toward him. I don't know why, but my mood has gone sour. I hope Rori isn't flirting with that chick. Fake girlfriend or not, I don't tolerate that kind of bullshit. When you're with me, I'm the queen. I don't share.

The little twist in my chest has nothing to do with jealousy. Why would I be jealous? Rori is nothing to me.

Halfway there, someone grabs my arm. I turn, ready to bite the idiot's head off, but it's Miles who stopped me. "Emma, wait a second. It's not what you think."

"I don't know what you're talking about."

"That woman Rori is talking to is his ex-girlfriend. They haven't seen each other in a long time."

I pull my arm from Miles's grasp, annoyed. Does he think giving me that information is supposed to mollify me? He's looking at me like I'm about to commit murder, so maybe I'm giving off that kind of vibe. I always despised this type of behavior in other women. Jealousy is nothing more than insecurity.

"Miles, what exactly do you think I was going to do? Pick a catfight with the woman?" I ask to save face.

He rubs the back of his neck and gives me a guilt-ridden expression. "Honestly, you looked a little murderous a second ago."

Shit. I'd better control my temper. This is all new to me. I've never formed any type of attachment with a guy before to get possessive. Maybe I *am* like those jealous women I laughed at. Wouldn't that be ironic?

"Anyway," Miles continues, "I thought I'd give you a little intel. I know you and Rori haven't been dating for a long time, but to be completely honest, I don't think Rori would ever talk about Alannah voluntarily."

"What happened between them?"

"It's not up to me to tell, but they dated throughout high school, and everyone thought they would end up getting married one day. But then...." Miles looks in Rori's direction and doesn't elaborate.

"God, Miles, if you're going to start telling a story, you'd better be prepared to go until the end."

"Let's just say Alannah left Rori when he needed her the most."

"That's just great," I mumble, more to myself than anyone else.

I leave Miles behind, my friendly disposition toward the guy seriously compromised. I can't believe he would blabber about Rori's past like that. I'd hate it if one of my friends did that to me.

I approach Rori and his ex just in time to hear her say she hasn't moved on. I see red and before I know it, I'm declaring open war. Fuck it. I *am* the crazy jealous girlfriend, even if I'm fake.

Rori turns to me, eyebrows raised. At least he doesn't look guilty.

"Who are you?" the bitchface asks, glaring at me from head to toe.

I wrap my arms around Rori's waist, getting really comfortable pressed against him. His strong arm covers my shoulder, making me melt, and also giving me a sense of victory. Emma one, ex-girlfriend minus ten.

"I'm Rori's girlfriend," I say with glee.

I make no attempt to hide the scrutinizing glance I give her, nor the judgmental bitchy look I've perfected over the years. I don't even have to pretend that I find her appearance lacking. She's one of those chicks who likes to combine sporty with sexy.

Too bad her overly tanned orange skin and heavy makeup are doing nothing to help her.

She turns to Rori with accusation in her eyes. "Since when do you have a girlfriend?"

"I fail to see how that's your business," Rori says.

"You know, Rori, I'm glad I dumped your sorry ass. Good riddance." She pushes me out of her way, and the only reason I don't show her why no one messes with Emma Hart is Rori's arm keeping me in place. But inside, I'm seething.

"I'm sorry about that. Lewis told her I was in town, and she tracked us via social media."

"Why did Lewis tell her?"

"He didn't mean to. They're cousins, and I guess he slipped the info by accident."

I'm still staring in the direction she disappeared to, hoping she'll come back so I can, I don't know, gouge her eyes out. Shit, I'm savage.

"She's awful," I say.

Rori doesn't offer a comment, so I turn to him, feeling a little bad. "I'm sorry. I know you guys dated for a long time in high school."

His eyes turn to slits. "How do you know that?"

"It seems all your friends have loose mouths. It was Miles. He stopped me on the way here to fill me in."

"What else did he tell you?" Rori's tone is harder, but I sense he's not mad at me.

"Just the basics. That you two dated, and then she broke up with you when you were going through a rough patch."

Rori rubs his face and looks away. "He shouldn't have said anything."

I pinch his chin between my forefinger and thumb, turning his face back to mine. "Hey, enough with the gloom. Let's try to get this evening back on track, shall we?"

He smiles and then, to my surprise, kisses me on the cheek.

Ah hell, he shouldn't have done that. My face bursts into flames, and every single cell in body seems to ignite. Breathless, I ask, "What was that for?"

"For putting up with my messes." He turns to the high table next to him and grabs two shot glasses. "Let's toast."

I don't need to take a whiff of the drink to know Rori got me whiskey. He already knows my taste. "Toast to what?"

"Hmm, to a fruitful manhunt and a drama-free wedding."

My heart sinks at Rori's mention of the main purpose of this trip. Finding Declan Kelly is becoming less and less important. But tonight, I'll pretend I'm not on a mission and try to have fun.

The fiery drink scratches my throat as it goes down, but the warmth that spreads through my limbs is worth it to vanquish the lingering remains of the panic attack.

"Got rid of her already, huh?" Lewis asks as he joins us, Miles and Dimitri in tow.

"I was about to when Emma showed up. Perfect timing." Rori winks at me.

"Fuck. I have to talk with Alannah. Showing up here like a stalker is crazy shit even for her." Lewis looks out in the distance.

"Forget it, mate." Rori claps his friend on the shoulder. "How about a game of pool? I haven't obliterated you in a while."

"Ha-ha. Only because I was stoned out of my mind the last time. What are the stakes tonight?"

"Whoever wins gets to kiss Emma," Dimitri jokes, but it's a terrible one.

"Not even in your dreams," I say at the same time Rori tells Dimitri to piss off.

"You're such a jackass." Miles glares at his idiotic friend.

"What? It was worth a try." The guy wobbles on his feet,

needing to brace against the edge of the pool table to avoid falling to the floor.

"How much have you drank already?" Rori asks.

"Not nearly enough." Dimitri laughs.

"I'm calling dibs on Rori," Miles shouts.

"Bloody fantastic. I might as well just hand you guys the money." Lewis throws his hands in the air.

"Hold up," I say. "What kind of sexist bullshit is that? I want to play."

Lewis glances at me. "How good are you? If you're better than drunken Dimitri, you're in. I have nothing against women playing, but you have to be able to hold your own. I hate losing money." He offers me the cue.

I grab it with a humph and sashay toward the table. "I hate losing money too." I turn to Rori. "Sorry, honey. Say bye-bye to your hard-earned cash."

Rori chalks up his cue without taking his eyes off me. God, why did that thought sound so dirty in my head?

"We'll see about that, *sweetie pie*." He smirks.

"For fuck's sake. Think of less barf-inducing nicknames for each other, will you?" Dimitri drops into a chair nearby, looking a little greener than before.

"I don't think that's what making you sick, mate." Miles laughs.

"How much are we betting?" I ask.

Lewis looks at Rori and shrugs. "A hundred each?"

"Sure. Miles?"

"I just got paid today and I'm feeling lucky. Let's do it."

Rori breaks, and so the game begins. He's very good, managing to get three in before missing the fourth shot. Lewis tells me to go next, but I know it's not chivalry that prompted him to do so. He wants to know how much of the weight I'm going to pull. I blow a kiss in Rori's direction before I position my cue on the table. I have to lean forward, which offers a better view of my cleavage to him and Miles. I hear whistles coming from behind, but a warning from Rori has the other guys piping down pretty quickly.

I'm dying to see the expression on Rori's face, but I can't allow myself to get distracted now. I focus on my aim and then bang, I hit the ball in a precise shot. It goes into the hole like a missile.

"Holy shit. The girl is good," Dimitri says in awe.

I glance at Rori, feeling pretty pleased with myself. I haven't lost my skills. He's smiling without teeth and his arms are crossed. It's his gaze that makes me weak in the knees, though. His eyes seem to sparkle with pride, and it creates pandemonium in my belly.

I shake my head, looking at the table again. That first ball was an easy shot, but now I have to analyze the position of the remaining ones, check all the angles, and do my calculations right. I circle the table before I make my selection. Once again, the ball flies into the hole. I should hold back, but I was never one to go easy when it came to any sort of competitive game. I like to win.

The first round is over in five minutes. Lewis is laughing like a maniac, already counting our win as dead certain.

"I can't believe this." Miles stares at the empty table with his hands on his hips. "Damn it, Rori. Why didn't you tell us your girlfriend was a master at pool?"

"Because he didn't know," Lewis answers before Rori can.

Grumbling, Rori chalks up again. "Well, now that I know, I won't go easy on you again."

Lewis bumps my arm with his elbow. "Your boyfriend is a sore loser, if you didn't already know."

"It suits me fine. I love a challenge." I smile at Rori, who in turn stares at me through slits. Shit. That predatorial glance is sexy as hell. I should stop with the crazy flirtation. It won't end well.

Rori and Miles win the next round, but only because Lewis gets distracted by a big-chested bimbo and misses an easy shot. I almost bite his head off. We're now playing the last round, and it's Rori's turn. I can already tell it's very unlikely he'll miss this shot, so I decide to see if Rori's focus is solid or if he can also be distracted by the opposite sex. While he's preparing to strike the ball, I sit on the high chair opposite him and cross my legs seductively, letting my skirt hike up. He glances up from his bent position, and I swear he's clenching his jaw harder now. Before he can collect his thoughts, I lace my hands over my knees and lean forward, giving him an excellent view of my sexy bra. Rori narrows his eyes, probably catching on that I'm doing it on purpose. With a slight shake of his head, he drops his gaze to the ball in front of him, but I can tell the angle of his stick is wrong. He misses the shot.

"Damn it!" He straightens up, glaring at the ball that didn't go in. Then he turns to me and walks around the table with purpose.

I don't get off the chair. It's Lewis's turn anyway. Rori stops in front of me, and I automatically uncross my legs as if I wanted to welcome him between them. *Not if. I do, I do.* Crap, I'm in so much trouble. He leans forward, bringing his lips close to mine.

"I know what you did," he whispers against my mouth, making it impossible for me to think straight. His hot breath on my skin gives me the worst kind of ideas. I want to be bad tonight.

"I don't know what you're talking about."

"Don't start something you can't finish, Em."

I lick my lips and Rori moves closer, his crotch now an inch away from mine. *Would it be completely inappropriate if I hooked my feet behind his legs? Yes, yes it would.* He brushes his nose on the crook of my neck, killing my resolve to keep things platonic between us. I want him, and I want him now.

"God, you smell good," he whispers, his voice husky and full of need.

This is it. I'm going in, consequences be damned.

"Oi, Rori," Lewis hollers from the other side of the table, and Rori pulls back as if he's been yanked by an elastic band that stretched too far.

"Quit the foreplay and pay up. You lost, mate," Lewis continues.

Rori turns to his friend and I'm left breathless, confused, and horny as fuck. The throbbing between my legs tells me it's time to bust out the vibrator when I get back to the hotel. I'm glad I always travel prepared, because I'm so not a fan of cold showers.

12
———

EMMA

My head is fuzzy, and I feel as giddy as a schoolgirl on her first date. But this isn't child's play—this is the real deal, and shit is about to go down. As I walk down the hallway ahead of Rori, I sense his hungry gaze scorching every inch of my body. I can't imagine what he'll do to me once we're inside my room.

I stop in front of the door and fiddle inside my purse, trying to get the keycard out. Rori places his hand against it and cages me in with his frame. His lemony scent envelopes me, permeating my senses. God, I don't know how I've been able to resist him until now. He brings his face closer and nuzzles my neck with his nose, then with his cheek. Unable to resist such teasing, I arch my spine backward, reaching for him. His free arm goes around my waist and brings me flush against his body.

"Rori," I whisper, melting like butter against him. I'm glad he's holding me in place, because my legs have lost their ability to hold me upright.

"Em." He bites my shoulder softly, eliciting a moan from me.

Then he grabs the keycard from my hand and swipes it in front of the reader. A soft beep announces the door is unlocked.

Rori turns the knob and together we enter the darkened room. He pushes me against the wall before the door even clicks shut and claims my mouth in a mind-blowing, savage kiss. My hands go around his neck, then up the back of his head until I find what I'm looking for. I pull his hairband off and Rori's glorious mane comes loose, framing his face.

"I love your hair," I whisper against his lips.

"I love your mouth," he replies before sweeping his tongue against mine again.

Fuck, the man knows how to kiss, but I'm ready for so much more. I stretch my arm out, searching for the light switch. I need to be able to see him, because it would be sacrilege to taste him without the view. The light comes on with a soft click, and thank fuck for low, dimmed settings. The entire room is bathed in an orange hue, setting the perfect atmosphere for some wicked games.

With great effort, I push Rori back. He stumbles as if in a daze and stares at me with the sexiest gaze I've ever seen on a man. My lips break into a sly grin as I begin to unbutton my shirt. Before I finish my task, Rori takes off his own T-shirt, tossing it to a corner.

Mama mia, I want to lick every inch of those abs.

I untie the knot holding my wrap dress in place, peeling it off my arms, and letting it fall where it does. Rori's gaze drops to my boobs and stays there for a moment. I run my fingers over their swell. "Like what you see?"

"Jesus, what kind of question is that?"

"How badly do you want to touch them?"

"Very, very badly." He takes a step forward but stops when I wag my finger.

"Hold up."

"Emma, please."

I smile from ear to ear, victorious. "You have to beg, on your knees."

My demand surprises him, but the hesitation only lasts a brief moment before he drops to the floor in front of me. "Please, Em. I'm begging you."

I walk to him, bending forward when I'm close enough. I pinch his chin between my fingers and bring his face up to mine. "Didn't I tell you, Rori?"

"Tell me what?"

"That if I truly wanted you in my bed, you would be on your knees, begging."

My eyes fly open as the irritating sound of my alarm blasts in the once-silent hotel room. I hit the Off button while I try to catch my breath. The other side of the bed is empty; I know without having to look. Disappointment washes over me, leaving me cold and bereft. It was a dream, a sexy and damn-realistic dream. My heart is still pounding, and my clit is throbbing like mad. I don't think anything but the real deal will satiate my hunger.

When I got back to the hotel last night, I busted out the bullet, but my little sex toy did nothing to quench the fire burning inside of me. And now that my imagination has stimulated all my senses, fat chance of it working now.

Stupid dream.

I'm glad I wised up and switched alcohol for water last night. My precaution had everything to do with Rori. It would be too easy to attack him and blame it on alcohol. There were too many close calls already. I have to be more careful.

One good thing about my decision is that I woke this morning hangover free and with enough disposition to go for a jog. Exercising religiously is the only way I can eat whatever I want and maintain my slim figure. I may be a skinny bitch, but I work hard for it.

When I return to the hotel, covered in sweat, I opt for the stairs to keep the cardio going—and also to avoid seeing anyone while looking like a drenched tomato. My cheeks inevitably get red whenever I do any high-impact activity. When I hit my floor, I slow down, pressing a finger against my neck to check my pulse.

The ping of the elevator ahead makes me look up. Rori steps out, wearing workout clothes that make my mouth drier than it already was. His muscle T-shirt is glued to his body, showing a physique that's meant to be worshipped in any way possible. I'm thinking hands and tongue. Memories of the dream flood my brain, and I'm afraid there's a neon sign above my head announcing my mind is in the gutter.

Rori's arms are corded with muscles, and there's only one word that comes to mind to describe them—*alpine*. He's a mountain I'd love to climb.

Whoa, dangerous thoughts, Emma. Dangerous and filthy.

"Good morning." He smiles.

"Morning." My voice is hoarse, so I clear my throat before I continue. "Good workout?"

Jesus, couldn't I think of anything else to say?

"Sure. Did you have a good run?" His eyes do I quick scan of my body, not lingering in any particular area before he looks at my face again.

"Yup." I force my legs to move. This conversation is doing my head in already. My body and brain are at war with one another.

"Maybe I'll join you next time."

No, no, no. I can't run with you, I want to say, but I keep my mouth shut and just nod.

"We should hit the road soon if we want to arrive in Kinsale early. It's over three hours' drive from here." He stops in front of his door and turns to me.

"Oh shoot," I say. "Our rental car. I totally forgot about it. We never got it at the airport."

"Don't worry. I called them yesterday and sorted it out. They have a pickup location not too far from here."

"Good." I flash my keycard in front of the scanner, but pause before opening the door all the way and glance at Rori. "Should we meet for breakfast in half an hour?"

"That's all you need? Thirty minutes?" He arches his eyebrows a little.

"Hey, I resent the implication. Unless *you* are the one who needs more time to deal with your tresses."

He chuckles, shaking his head. "Nope. I'll see you in thirty."

I don't realize I'm still frozen on the spot until Rori walks into his room and closes the door. I really need to get my act together. But it seems the sane part of my brain decided to take a vacation, leaving the naughty side in charge.

As I take my clothes off, I begin to picture Rori doing the same thing, and that doesn't help my case one bit. I don't think a cold shower will suffice; maybe I'll need to use my vibrator again. On the other hand, it might not be a good idea to see the guy in such a short period of time after I climax fantasizing about him. What a dilemma.

I try to think of mundane things as I shower, but when my fingers touch my clit, all I can think about is Rori and how I wish he was the one touching me. I stroke myself slowly as I give in to the fantasy. I'm not sure what I would prefer, Rori's fingers between my legs or his mouth. Probably both at the same time. I close my eyes and throw my head back, letting the hot jet of water hit my face while the tension builds down below. Like last night, I climax within a minute, biting my lower lip to avoid moaning out loud. I have no idea how thin these walls are.

My breathing is a little shallow when I turn off the water, and the bathroom is enveloped in steam. I wipe the foggy mirror, and it's not a surprise when the reflection there shows my flushed cheeks. I stare hard at myself as I vow silently to take control of the situation.

You can do this, Emma.

An itching on my foot distracts me from my internal pep talk. I glance down and let out a yelp when I see the huge spider crawling over it. On reflex, I jump backward, trying to dislodge it. The spider falls to the floor, but so do I, hitting my elbow on the toilet seat hard. I scream again, much louder this time, holding my arm close to my body as white-hot pain shoots up my limb.

Damn it, I hope I didn't break anything.

It takes a few seconds for Rori to bang on the door linking our rooms. I guess I have my answer about the walls. He would've been able to hear me if I had moaned out loud as I climaxed.

With a groan, I push myself off the ground using my good hand while I search for the eight-legged freak responsible for this.

"Emma, please say something or I'll bring this door down."

"I'm okay," I choke out, pain lacing my words. I pull the bathrobe from its peg behind the bathroom door, but I can't move my arm. It hurts too much. This is so not good.

"You don't sound okay. What happened?" Rori insists.

I push my good arm through the hole first, and then I throw the other side of the robe over my shoulder. I can't tie the sash, so I try my best to keep the opening closed with my hand. It's not ideal, but it's the best I can do. I check that most of my body is covered before I unlock the internal door for Rori.

Holy shit. He must've been in the shower when he heard me, because his hair is loose and soaking wet. He's wrapped a towel around his waist, giving me a perfect view of his wide, naked chest and the droplets of water glistening there.

That's it. He just became my real-life fantasy. No matter what happens when I find Declan, Rori will always plague my mind. He's not Tarzan—he's Adonis on Earth.

His eyes do a quick scan of me, his furrowed brows creating a deep V on his forehead. "What happened?"

"There was a spider." His mouth makes a little O, so before he makes an obnoxious comment, I continue. "For your information, it was humungous, so I got spooked and ended up slipping on the wet floor. I hit my elbow on the toilet bowl. Nothing major."

"Nothing major, huh? Is that why you're cradling your arm like that? Let me take a look."

"No way!" I take a step back. "I'm naked underneath the robe."

That gives Rori pause. Now he's looking at everything but me. "Can you move your arm at all?"

I try stretching it, but the pain increases when I do so. "Nope." It seems I won't have a choice. "Okay, turn around. I think I can put my panties and bra on at least."

Rori does as I ask, and I quickly grab the panties I had already laid on the bed. Putting them on with only one arm and trying to keep the robe from slipping is the most awkward thing I've done in a while. I hope Rori is keeping his end of the bargain and not looking. I'm glad the bra I chose—a hot pink number with black lace details—isn't the most outrageous piece of lingerie I own. It might be super-sexy for some people, but I don't buy boring cotton underwear, so this can be classified as tame for me—my nipples don't show in it. Slowly, I loop my wounded arm though the strap, then do the same with the other. But the closing the hook part will be a little trickier.

I look over my shoulder and say, "Would you mind helping here?"

He turns, his gaze zeroing on my naked back. "Sure."

I look forward again, trying to suppress a shiver when he stops behind me awfully close. His fingers are a little cold, and when they brush against my skin, goose bumps form everywhere. Hell and damn. His touch is ten thousand times better in real life.

With the clasp closed, I take a deep breath and pivot, still cradling my arm against my body. Rori glances down, his gaze traveling quickly over the swell of my breasts before focusing on my arm. I watch his face closely, wondering if he's feeling the tension in the air like I am. Yesterday we were so close to kissing, but extenuating circumstances—aka, the appearance of the ex-love of his life, and my panic attack—gave both of us the perfect excuse to brush off the moment as inconsequential. Today, there's no excuse, only an undeniable physical attraction —at least on my side.

With an extremely gentle touch, Rori takes my injured arm into his hands. I whimper when he tries to unbend it.

"Sorry," he says. "It's already getting swollen. We'll need to get that checked."

The air exits my lungs in a powerful gale, loaded with annoyance. "I was afraid of that. Great way to start our journey. Stupid spider."

"Hey, stuff happens. No worries. Now, what were you planning to wear? I'll help you get dressed."

Biting my lip, I nod in the bed's direction. "The black sweater over there, but I don't think I can manage pulling my arm through the hole, even with your help."

"All right. Did you bring any button-down shirts?"

"Yes, but they're all long-sleeved. Hmm, I think I brought a vest. That could work."

Rori turns to my suitcase and starts to move things around. The organization freak in me winces as if in pain. There's nothing I hate more than piles of tangled clothes. To forget my Monica Geller tendencies, I allow myself to appreciate the fine specimen that is Rori O'Shea. My eyes roam freely over his body, committing every detail of his backside to memory. His muscles are like valleys, sinuous and beautiful. And his ass, don't get me started on his ass. The towel doesn't do much to conceal that he has a yummy booty. I'm craving this man; I'm craving him bad.

Gorgeous guys like him are—*were*—my addiction, and if I intend to keep my promise, I can't go down the rabbit hole.

Rori finally swings around, holding the cute vest I was lucky to have packed. It's snug and the fabric is a little shimmery. It's meant for going out, but it'll do for now.

"That's the one," I say.

"This is very fine, not suitable for winter. You'll be cold." He returns with vest in hand, but his eyes don't stray from my face once. He's acting like the perfect gentleman. I guess I should be glad for his consideration, but honestly, my ego is a little bruised that he's not trying to sneak a peek.

"I'll wear my fleece-lined coat."

I let go of my injured arm and let Rori help me with the vest, wincing at the slightest movement. He's once again all over my personal space, and all I can think about is the heat emanating from his body, the intoxicating smell of his lemony shampoo. This must be a test of my resolve.

Rori freezes when it comes to the buttoning part. His eyes aren't aimed at my breasts though, but at the horrible scar etched on my skin. Ah fuck. I completely forgot about it, which says a lot about my current state of my mind. I don't ever let anyone see it, not even my closest friends. I don't wear bikinis anymore, and I always keep my top on during sex.

I hastily pull both sides of the vest close together, hiding my scar from view.

"You don't need to hide it from me," Rori says softly.

"I never let anyone see it. It's—never mind." I look away.

"It's okay. I barely got a glimpse."

I know he's lying, but I don't call him on it. He finishes his task without another word.

"Thanks. I think I can manage putting my pants on."

"Okay, holler if you need anything. I'll leave my door unlocked."

He returns to his room and I can finally breathe properly.

Putting my jeans on is harder than the panties were, mainly because I only own the snug type. Damn it. Why didn't I pack boyfriend jeans? Oh, that's right, because I don't have any.

I call Rori back into my room once I'm fully dressed so he can help me with my luggage. I don't bother blow-drying my hair, choosing to hide it under a woolen hat and hope it'll keep my head warm.

"Let's not worry about checking out now and get you to an emergency room first." Rori grabs my coat and throws it around my shoulders without being asked to do so. He buttons the top as if I were a little child, then loops my thick scarf around my neck. I feel like a snowman now.

"Gee, is this really necessary? It wasn't that cold earlier."

"Do you want to catch a cold on top of a busted arm?"

I watch him through slits. "That's not how you catch a cold. Viruses are involved."

"Right, try standing outside wearing only your knickers and see if you don't fall sick."

He turns to the door, missing when I stick my tongue out at him. I've never had a mother or grandmother around, but I can imagine that's something one of them would say.

We hop into a cab, the ride to the nearest hospital taking around ten minutes. My arm is still throbbing, but it only hurts really bad when I'm jostled, which happens every two minutes or so.

"How long do you think it'll take for a doctor to see me?" I ask right before we enter the hospital.

"It really depends on the day. Just make sure you don't play tough and hide your pain."

The waiting room is relatively empty, which surprises me. I've been to the emergency room in LA once when a guy I was seeing accidentally stapled his forehead. It was a zoo, and we had to wait for three hours before he was seen.

Rori ushers me to the reception desk with his hand on my

lower back, and even though there are layers of clothing between us, his touch brands me. I don't know how I'm going to resist jumping the guy. My only hope is that I find Declan right away when we arrive in Kinsale.

But what if there are no magical sparks?

No, I can't think like that. It's not only my promise to Dad that's preventing me from seducing Rori. I'm beginning to like him as a friend, and I know once sex is in the equation, it ruins everything. No, not the sex part—*I'll* ruin everything. I'm a man-eater, after all.

When the receptionist asks the problem, Rori doesn't answer for me like I know most guys would, thinking they were helping. I tell her the bare minimum, skipping the part about the spider. I fell and hit my elbow on the toilet bowl. That's all she cares about anyway. When she asks me about the amount of pain, I don't lie. It hurts, but it's not excruciating.

"Please take a seat. We'll call your name shortly."

"How shortly?" Rori asks before I can.

"Right now, probably half an hour."

Okay, not too bad.

As I sit next to Rori, I feel like a dwarf in comparison. His legs seem to go on for miles, and they're as thick as tree trunks. I only got a peek of his calves earlier, but honestly, I wasn't really paying attention to his bottom half. His back and his ass kept distracting me.

"Last night went well, despite some hiccups," I say to distract myself.

"Yup. You play a pretty convincing girlfriend." Rori chuckles.

"Can I ask you a question?"

"Sure."

"What happened between you and Alannah?"

Rori shifts in his seat, and I sense I've entered forbidden

territory. "What do you mean?" he asks, his tone a little harsher.

"Well, I know you dated her throughout high school, but there seemed to be some unresolved issue between the two of you."

"The only thing unresolved is that Alannah is still hung up on the past."

"Nine years is a long time to be hung up on someone. But I guess it's quite normal when it comes to your first serious relationship."

"Are you still hung up on your first boyfriend?" Rori turns to me, but I don't look into his eyes, choosing to drop my gaze to my lap instead.

"I never had a boyfriend."

He doesn't speak for several beats, and that makes me curious. I glance up to find him staring at me, his jaw slack.

"What?" I ask.

"You're joking, right?" The incredulous glint in his eyes is almost comical.

"No. I've never been in a relationship. I've never fallen in love either."

Rori narrows his eyes, as if my answer displeases him somehow. "What makes you think this guy Declan will be any different?"

I take a deep breath and decide that now is as good time as any to tell Rori about my not-so-great past.

"Do you remember the terrorist attack in Brussels last year?"

"The one in the metro? Yeah."

"Well, I was in the train with the bomb."

Nothing comes from Rori except stunned silence. I search his eyes, almost certain I'll find pity there, but that's not what I read in his gaze. First is surprise, and then anger. He reaches out and covers my hand with his.

"Emma, I'm so sorry. I had no idea."

"It's okay. Not many people do. I don't like to talk about it, and it's also the reason I don't flaunt my scar."

"That's why you didn't want to go down to the bar last night. Em, you should've told me."

The worry in his tone does something to my heart. I can't explain it. It's not exactly a fuzzy feeling, but it definitely helps ease some of the pressure in my chest.

"My therapist says I have to face my fears to be rid of them. She'll be happy to learn I managed to go underground."

"How does Declan fit in with all this?"

"He saved me that day. My wounds were severe. I couldn't move. He pulled me out of the debris and helped get me to the surface. I'd be dead if it weren't for him."

"I see." Rori stares ahead and locks his jaw tight. I wish I knew what he's thinking.

"It's not completely random," I feel the need to add. "We were on the same train almost every morning. That day had been the first time we actually got to talk and then... *hell*."

Rori squeezes my hand gently, grounding me, preventing me from going too deep in those memories.

"He didn't come visit you in the hospital?"

"If he wanted to do so, I don't think he could find me. I was told it was complete madness in the city and finding loved ones was extremely difficult."

Suddenly, Rori lets go of my hand and rubs his face. "I'm glad he helped you. Declan Kelly is indeed a hero, but this is the part you're probably not going to like to hear." He pauses and turns to me, his stare a little harder than before. "I don't understand your logic."

I flatten my lips, taking Rori's comment as criticism. "I've never fallen in love before. I actually don't think I *can* fall in love. But if I have any chance of succumbing to the feeling my friends all have, it has to be with someone I already have *some* connection with, even if it's tragic."

Rori rests his elbows on his knees and stares forward. He doesn't make any more comments, and that unnerves me. He's definitely judging me.

"I know you think I'm nuts," I say.

He glances in my direction again, eyebrows furrowed and lips flat. "I don't. I sincerely hope you find this guy and he's everything you want him to be."

"Are you being sarcastic now?"

He shakes his head. "Nope."

I narrow my eyes because I don't believe a word coming out of his mouth. God, I would be judging me if I were in his shoes.

I open my mouth to argue, but my name is called and the moment is gone. Rori doesn't move from his chair. At least he has the common sense to know I don't want him around right now.

13

RORI

SHIT, I WAS NOT EXPECTING SUCH A CONFESSION FROM EMMA. I thought the scar was the result of a car accident, not a terrorist attack. No wonder she panicked before going into that underground pub. I can't believe she actually managed to conquer her fear and have a good time in the end.

The more I get to know her, the more in awe I become, and I totally blew it just now. She thinks I'm judging her, and despite my denial, maybe I am. From the get-go, I thought her idea was a little crazy, but now, knowing more details, it's impossible not to judge. I don't need to see into the future to know her plan will backfire. Or maybe I secretly want her to fail, and isn't that just fucking great.

One thing I can't deny. I'm accumulating a lot of feelings toward the girl. There's attraction. It's pretty fucking obvious when only being near her puts me in overdrive. My hands are getting calluses from all the extra work.

And things are about to get more complicated when we arrive in Kinsale. I received a text from my sister this morning, and it seems the harmless lie I told my friends yesterday has reached the little village I used to call home. Now my entire family thinks Emma is my girlfriend. I have no bloody clue how I'm going to break the news to her. She'll go mental, no doubt.

An hour later, she comes out with her arm in a sling. Standing up, I watch her face closely, trying to gauge how mad she still is at me.

"It's not broken, only sprained," she says. "But I have to keep my arm immobilized for a week."

"That's good news. Emma, about before—"

"Drop it, Rori." She raises her good arm while staring daggers at me. "I don't care if you were judging me or not. You're entitled to your opinions, and honestly, they're nothing to me. I've never in my life cared about what others thought about me, and I'm not going to start now." She points to the door. "Shall we?"

Yeah, she's still pissed. I'd better wait until we're near Kinsale to break the news.

It took us another hour to hit the road out of the city. Since it was nearing lunchtime, I suggested we grab sandwiches and other snacks to go. We were supposed to be nearly there already, and it's a miracle my mother hasn't called yet to find out where we are.

The first hour of the trip is painfully quiet despite the music from the radio filling the void. The tension is killing me. I've lost count of how many times I opened and shut my mouth, ready to start a conversation, but changed my mind in the last second.

Emma's alternated between texting on her phone and looking out the window. It's a breathtaking view, but I wonder if she's actually appreciating anything. I had almost forgotten how beautiful Ireland is, with its northern coastal climate and the peaks and valleys mostly formed by ancient volcanoes. I'm about to suggest we stop in Cashel since we're already off schedule as it is when the music is interrupted by the sound of my phone ringing. My mother's name appears on the dashboard.

For fuck's sake. I must've paired my phone with the car's audio when I was messing with the navigation system earlier.

I press the Answer button and Mum's voice comes through the speakers, loud and demanding. "Rori, for heaven's sake. Where are you? I was expecting you two hours ago."

"Sorry, Mum. We got delayed."

Emma sits straighter in her seat and turns away from watching the landscape fly by.

"I prepared a lovely lunch, and we had the entire family waiting for you. Why didn't you call? Never mind. If you couldn't be bothered to tell your own mother that you were bringing a girlfriend, this behavior is not a surprise."

Fuuuck. I don't need to glance in Emma's direction to know she's glaring at me.

"Mum, you're on speaker."

"Oh, I am? Is Emma next to you?"

I rub my face and peel my eyes from the road for a split second to gauge Emma's reaction. She's no longer glaring—now she's smirking at me with a hint of satisfaction in her eyes. She's loving my imminent demise.

"Of course. Where else would she be?"

"Hi, Mrs. O'Shea," Emma says in an extra-sweet voice.

"Oh dear. Hello, honey. Please forgive my son. He fell onto his head when he was little. It's the only explanation I can give for his atrocious behavior. Mind you that we had arranged for you to sleep with Lizzy, but now that I know the truth, well, I have to make other arrangements."

"Please, Mrs. O'Shea. Don't trouble yourself. It's not a big deal if Rori and I don't share a room. It's only ten days. We'll survive."

"Nonsense, dear. It doesn't get more romantic than Ireland.

You two need your privacy. We're Catholics but we aren't prudes."

I turn to Emma again and find her flush-faced and flat-lipped. I mouth, "I'm sorry," which only makes her narrow her eyes.

"So, what time are you getting here?" Mum continues.

"We have two more hours to go."

"Two hours? That long? Oh okay, I guess I'll put the food away, then. Since you're already late, why don't you stop in Cashel? I'm sure Emma would love to visit St. Patrick's Rock."

I chance another look at her, a question in my gaze, noting how her angry expression has softened a bit. Maybe she's not as mad at me as she was before. She holds my stare, and then things become crystal clear as a hint of defiance flashes in her eyes.

"I'd love to visit Cashel," she says.

"You're going to love it," Mum replies.

Before she can add anything else that might give Emma more reason to be angry, I jump into the conversation. "I'll call you when we're done there."

"You'd better. See you soon, and drive safely."

"Thanks, Mum. I can't wait to see everyone."

The line goes silent for a second before the radio jumps back on.

"What the hell, Rori. Your family thinks we're together?"

"I didn't tell her," I say lamely. "Miles posted something on social media, and my little sister saw. I'm sorry."

"How am I supposed to look for Declan now?"

Of course. This whole blowup had to be about that damn hero. I'm beginning to hate the name Declan.

I grind my molars, then say, "I don't see how that's going to affect anything."

"Oh really, you don't? I came all the way here to find my

soul mate, and now I'm suddenly attached to you against my will."

"*Soul mate?*" I can't help the bitter laugh that escapes my lips. My fingers curl tighter around the steering wheel and I lock my jaw tight. Not that Emma doesn't have the right to be angry, but she didn't need to make it sound like being my fake girlfriend was a death sentence.

"If you're going to be such an insufferable ass during the entire trip, then you'd better just drop me off in the next town. I can look for Declan on my own."

"Calm down, will you? I didn't mean to laugh." *No, I'm just hiding how much I'm hating this entire arrangement.* "And don't worry about my family. I'll tell them the truth once we get there."

"Dimitri wasn't even that bad," she continues as if I hadn't spoken. "This mess was all for nothing."

"I said I'll fix it," I reply through clenched teeth. "Don't worry, no one will stay between you and your precious Declan, wherever he may be."

"I don't appreciate your tone."

I bite my tongue and don't reply right away. I need to cool down before I create an even bigger chasm between Emma and me.

The silence stretches through minutes. Emma's body is partially turned to the window and I can't see her face. My stomach twists into knots, something I haven't felt since I was a young lad. I can try to deny it as much as I want, but this irritation toward a man I don't know, and the feeling I'm losing something vital, has a name. Jealousy. I'm fucking jealous that Emma is after some illusion, a mere stranger. Isn't that ironic? Not too long ago, I turned her down, and now I'm wanting what? A second chance?

"I'm sorry, Emma," I finally say. "I messed up. I didn't think my little lie would travel all the way to Kinsale."

Emma switches her attention to me, her lips pursed. "This trip can't be for nothing, Rori. I can't fail."

"What if you can't find Declan, or worse, what if you do and he's not what you expect him to be?"

She doesn't answer right away, and I have to force myself to keep my eyes on the road, to ignore the sudden lurch in my chest.

"I have no idea." The reply leaves her lips in a soft whisper, as if she really didn't want to answer. "And the worst part of it all is that for the first time in my life, I don't have a plan B."

Why not me? The random thought pops in my head out of the blue, and I immediately stomp on it. I was hurt once by someone I loved deeply; I don't need to experience that heartache again.

And Emma will eat me whole and spit me out if I let her, of that I'm certain.

14

———

EMMA

I'M ANGRY, I'M UPSET WITH THE DELAY, MY ARM IS BOTHERING ME, but mostly I don't know what to do with the turmoil in my chest. Rori sounded almost jealous an hour ago when I mentioned Declan. Why? He can't be developing feelings for me, can he? I haven't done nothing to warrant that. Resolute that I am to be good on this trip, I didn't pull any of my stunts or use any of my seduction cards—at least, not on purpose.

No, it can't be. Rori was never one for me. He never noticed me before, and the only reason he did so the last time was because I was an inconvenience.

He slows down as we approach the famous site, Rock of Cashel. Sitting at the top of a hill, the twelfth-century construction is something straight out of a medieval movie. I feel like I've been transported back in time, and I'm not even out of the car yet.

"There it is," Rori says, leaning forward and closer to the windshield to stare better at the big castle up ahead. "Carraig Phádraig."

A shiver runs down my spine upon hearing those words coming out of his mouth. A caress wouldn't have felt so alluring. I've purposely not let his accent get to me, but it's impossible to ignore it when he brings out the Irish.

I'm out of the car before he even has the chance to shut off the engine. I don't wait for him as I head for the path that goes up to the castle, needing to put as much distance between us as possible.

A chilly gust of wind sweeps my hair, and random strands whip against my face, making it hard to see. My hand is busy holding my coat, so I drop my chin and brace the weather. To ward off the cold, I grab the end of my coat's lapels, trying to keep it closed. The sling gets in the way though, and by the time I reach the top of the hill, my teeth are chattering.

"Emma, wait up." Rori touches my shoulder and I jump, not expecting to see him so close.

"Where the hell did you come from?"

"I was right behind you. I called your name three times."

"What for? Didn't you get the hint that I wanted to be alone?"

Without replying, Rori throws a thick wool blanket over my shoulders, arranging it in a way that it will stay put despite the wind. I'm not instantly toasty, but I *am* warmer, in more ways than one. I make the mistake to look at his face, into his eyes that out here, under the open sky with the sun shining, are more green than hazel. God, he's so beautiful it physically hurts. Why must he be the culmination of all my fantasies wrapped up in this delicious package? *Why?*

He steps back and turns to glance at the castle. I realize then that I didn't thank him for his kindness, but before I can do so, he walks away in the opposite direction.

"Where are you going?"

He looks over his shoulder without pausing. "You said you wanted to be alone. I'm respecting your wishes."

I clamp my mouth shut, even though I feel like an idiot now. I don't want to be alone, not by any stretch. I want his company, even if all I do is glare at him. With a humph, I enter the line to pay for admission. It moves fast enough, but by the time it's my turn to pay, there's a huge lump stuck in my throat and my voice comes out strangled as a result. The cashier's bushy eyebrows furrow at me, concern shining in his gaze.

"Is everything all right, miss?"

"Yes, of course."

"Whoever he is, he's not worth crying about," the elderly man says with a tone of wisdom.

My jaw drops of its own accord. What the hell is he talking about? I give him the cash and grab my ticket with a jerky movement while several choice words run through my head. It's not until I feel an extra chill on my face that his comment makes sense. I touch my cheek and sure enough, there's moisture there.

What the actual fuck. I was crying? And over Rori?

I walk away from the crowd, looking for a corner where I can freak out properly. I never, ever cry. The last time I let someone get to me like that was... oh my God, in middle school when a boy I liked picked on me.

That's it. Rori and his judgmental opinions are what triggered the tears. I'm not losing my mind completely, only a little.

I'm ready to tour the castle—that's why I came here, after all—when a loud boom echoes all around me and knocks my world completely off its axis. My lungs seize and my heart stops beating for a split second before it restarts with a painful lurch.

I take several steps back until my body meets a stony wall. Rock of Cashel and all the tourists vanish from my sight, and are replaced by awful memories that take over all my senses. The acrid smell of smoke mixed with the stench of burned flesh turns my stomach upside down. My breathing is coming out in gasps, the muscles in my legs locked tight. I can't move, can't do anything besides stay frozen in an eternal state of impotence and panic.

I'm not sure how long I stay in that spot, barely maintaining my grip on reality, when Rori finds me. It takes me a moment to actually see him, standing in front of me. His hands are on my forearms, and he's shaking me a little. When his face finally comes into focus, I crush my body against his, forgetting the sprained arm. There's no pain, or maybe I'm so out of it that my brain can't process the stimulus.

Rori's arm goes around me, pulling me closer and creating a protective cocoon that's all warmth and safety. I need him to steady me, to be my anchor in the here and now, not in the past. I can't be trapped in that nightmare; I won't be able to keep my sanity.

Rori touches my lower back and whispers close to my ear. "Em, it's okay, just focus on breathing. You've got this."

It's not his words that help me regain control of my body but his voice, rough and sweet at the same time. I latch on to how Rori makes me feel, how every time he comes near me it gets harder to resist the pull. I fixate my mind on the memory of our kiss in my dream, and then finally my heart begins to slow down and I can breathe more easily.

"It's okay. I'm here. I'm here," he whispers softly.

"There was this loud noise, and—"

"I know. That's why I came. Some idiots decided to shoot fireworks as a prank."

I burrow my face against his chest, loving his clean scent of soap, shampoo, and aftershave, but not the fancy kind. It's simple like he is, but so, so dangerous to me.

"Let's get out of here," he says.

I don't say a word, just let him take me away. I can't remember anymore why I got so ticked off at him. Time and time again, Rori's come through when I needed him the most. I don't notice anything as we take the path back down to the car, so wrapped up that I am in everything Rori. His strong arms, his breathing, the way the light shines in his hair, revealing cooper and gold strands I hadn't noticed before. My heart skips a beat, and I have no clue why.

Once back in the car, Rori has to eventually let me go. My body revolts with the separation, the shaking renewing, but I want to prove to him that I'm not weak, that I can control my emotions. I watch him as he slides behind the wheel, his massive body taking up most of the space. More than ever I'm aware of his presence, how I'm drawn to him like he's a magnet and I'm steel.

We both turn in our seats simultaneously and face each other. All at once the air becomes thick and charged. I don't know who moves first, me or him, but we meet in the middle and stop only when our lips are a breath apart. Rori palms my cheek and breathes out my name.

I ignore all the warning bells, lock away all my logical arguments, and succumb to the desire running rampant in my veins. I breach the distance and kiss him, and in an instant I'm on fire. Rori's hand moves from my cheek to the back of my head, pulling me closer as his tongue delves deeper, curious and demanding. I whimper against his lips and he pulls back, staring into my eyes.

His breathing is shallow just like mine.

"Is this okay?" he whispers, his voice loaded with need.

"Yes, more than okay." My reply is just as breathless. I bring my lips back to his again and let myself be carried away by the brush of his tongue against mine, by the feel of his hand on my skin. This is the most innocent make-out session I've had in a long time, but it's the most erotic thing I've done as well.

I could stay in this car kissing Rori O'Shea forever.

15

EMMA

Nothing lasts forever. The pesky sound of a cell phone ringing bursts my bubble of bliss and the reality comes crashing in. Rori pulls back, all the way to his side of the car this time, and I feel like I've lost something in the process. I also return to my seat and try to fix my hair. It's tangled from Rori's fingers in it, and smoothing it out is impossible. Just as impossible as ignoring the tingling on my lips, and the throbbing between my legs.

Oh my God. What have I done? I can't even look at him right now.

He's on the phone, and by his replies, my guess is that he's talking with whoever he left in charge of his pub. The call doesn't last long, maybe three minutes tops, and when Rori presses the End button, he keeps staring at the device in his hand, as if he's having trouble looking at me as well.

I'm not far enough down the rabbit hole yet to not recognize that the longer this silence stretches, the worse it'll become.

"Thank you," I say.

He glances my way with an eyebrow raised. "Thank you? For what?"

"For distracting me from the panic. It helped big-time." My lie feels heavy in my chest. I know he didn't kiss me in order to distract me. Nor did I kiss him back for that reason. But what else can I say? I need to do damage control here, and giving another reason for our lack control is the best I can come up with.

Rori stares at me for the longest time, his gaze hard as if he's sniffing my bullshit. Then he glances forward, and with jaw tight, he says, "You're welcome."

The engine turns to life and off we go again, back on the road to meet his family.

To meet his family. Me. As his girlfriend.

Gah, I'm back to panicking for entire different reasons now. Butterflies on acid decide to wreak havoc in my belly. I've never had a serious boyfriend, and therefore I never had to meet any parents—and this little detail is making me nervous like hell, as ridiculous as it sounds. Rori promised to clear up the confusion, so in theory I have nothing to worry about, but the feeling of apprehension won't go away. I'm such a basket case it's not even funny. Maybe I should've gone to therapy way before my accident, just like most of my friends in high school did.

I have a huge lump in my throat by the time we pass the sign announcing Kinsale is the next exit, but when Rori keeps driving past it, I throw him a glance.

"You just missed our exit."

"Nope."

"You said your family lived in Kinsale."

"I said I was from Kinsale, but I never said my parents lived in the city. They own a bed-and-breakfast fifteen kilometers or so from the city, a farmhouse. I thought I told you that."

"You said they owned a farmhouse, but you never mentioned it wasn't in the city!"

"Jesus, it's just a technicality. Many people consider that area to be a part of Kinsale. Why are you mad?"

Exactly, why am I mad? No good reason besides nerves. But I won't tell Rori that.

"Because you keep withholding information from me. I should've come alone." The last part was just me being overly dramatic to hide the fact that I'm freaking out.

"Maybe you should have," he grumbles.

Ah, damn it. Now he's angry at me. *Way to go, Emma.*

I should apologize, but then I have to admit that I'm nervous. He's going to make fun of me, no doubt. I bite my tongue and look out the window. Soon, the stunning view leaves me speechless anyway: a lovely river framed by green valleys, and out in the distance a deep red farm building looms on the horizon. When Rori mentioned a farmhouse, I wasn't expecting this. A set of tall stone walls on each side of the road holds the wrought iron gate that opens to the property. On the left side is a sign: 'O'Shea Farmhouse Bed & Breakfast.'

I feel a little sick.

Rori parks the car in the only spot left, which is a little farther way from the main entrance, and then turns to me. "I'll make this painless, I promise. I'll go in first and clear the misunderstanding."

"Okay."

A loud knock on my window has me jumping in my seat. There's a young, toothless kid outside grinning from ear to ear.

"Jesus." I place my hand over my chest.

The kid laughs maniacally before running away. Outside, I hear a woman's voice scolding him.

"Ah, shit. So much for going in alone," Rori mumbles.

A busty woman with flaming red hair is outside his door, trying to peer inside the car. "Come on out, Rori. Let me see you."

With an apologetic sigh, he glances at me. "This is my aunt Wilma."

Seeing the guilt in his gaze mollifies me. He really didn't mean for things to go this far. I decide put him out of his misery; I'll go on with the charade for a little longer.

Decision made, I get out of the car and walk over to Aunt Wilma.

"Hi. I'm Emma Hart." I extend my hand.

Instead of shaking it, the woman places both hands over her chest as she gets teary-eyed. "Oh my goodness. You're gorgeous. Come here. Give me a hug."

She engulfs me in the mother of bear hugs and squeezes me so tightly I can barely breathe. Tears form in my eyes as well, not because of emotion but pain. She didn't even see the sling.

"Auntie. Watch her arm."

Rori pulls the woman back and I let out a shaky breath. My arm is throbbing just as a bad as it did when I hit the toilet bowl.

"Oh dear. You poor thing. I didn't even see your arm was in a sling. I was so excited to finally meet you."

"Wilma, what's all that racket?" a newcomer asks.

"Rori's here." His aunt looks over her shoulder.

A slimmer version of Wilma comes running down the driveway and practically jumps into Rori's arms. "You're finally here. I can't believe it."

"Hi, Mum."

They hug for a few seconds, and after a moment I notice both of them are shaking. His mother is definitely crying, but is he?

She finally steps away and turns to me, wiping away her tears. "You must be Emma." Her gaze drops to my arm and her eyes widen. "What happened?"

"I fell in the bathroom." I feel my cheeks warming. "It's the reason we're late. I'm so sorry."

"There's nothing to be sorry about." She throws her arm over my shoulder and kisses my forehead, surprising the heck out of me. Not even my father is prone to such open displays of affection.

"Come on now," she continues. "The entire family is dying to meet you. Rori hasn't been home in six years, and I don't think he ever mentioned having a girlfriend in all the time he's been living in California. You must be something special indeed."

I let Rori's mom drag me toward the house, but not before I throw an incredulous look at him. He never dated seriously since breaking up with that horrid woman I had the displeasure of meeting last night? How is that possible? A person doesn't go from being in a fully committed relationship to casual dating unless he's been hurt deeply. I'm hit by an urge to kick the hell out of his ex. How can you have this guy and throw him away?

Whoa. Danger, danger, Will Robinson. It sounds like I want to replace the woman in Rori's heart, which is not what I want at all.

Or is it?

I feel a pang in my chest, as if there's a dagger twisting in there. Jealousy. I'm suffering from retroactive jealousy. I'm fucking losing it.

Before I know it, we're crossing through the front door, where the smell of delicious food wafts through my nose. Loud voices come from a room to my right, and the butterflies I felt during the car ride come back with a vengeance.

"Look who I found outside," Rori's mom announces, and all eyes turn to us.

"Rori!" A teenage girl with strawberry-blonde hair jumps

from the couch and crosses the room with her long legs. "I can't believe you're here."

She leaps into her big brother's arms, and again I see how the encounter affects Rori. I don't get it. If he's that close to his family, how come he doesn't visit more often? It can't be only because he doesn't want to bump into his ex, not when he seems to loathe her. There must be another reason.

The rest of his family takes turns hugging him, and then me by default. My face is hurting from smiling ear to ear after I'm introduced to everyone. I used the trick I was taught by my father to always repeat someone's name as I'm introduced—it's easier to remember it later—but I'm not sure if it'll work today.

Rori's father's name is Gerard, which I immediately associated with Gerard Butler. He has thick straw-colored hair like his son, but it's cut short and is salted with gray here and there. Put side by side, there's no denying they're father and son. Rori takes almost everything from his dad, from the tall frame to the bone structure.

His mother, Anne O'Shea, is not as bad as I thought based on her earlier exchange on the phone with Rori. I pegged her to be a helicopter mom, but it's clear that her sister Wilma is ten times worse, fussing over everything and talking nonstop. Or maybe Rori's mother doesn't think I'm good enough for her son, hence why she's holding back. The smile on my face wilts and my stomach clenches painfully just thinking about the possibility.

Why are you worrying about that, Emma? Rori isn't your boyfriend.

I need to hold myself together. I'm sounding like an immature teenager, not the decisive woman I actually am. I'm twenty-two years old, for crying out loud, not sixteen.

Wilma's husband says something to Rori that makes him laugh from the belly up. I can't help but stare while millions of butterflies take formation in my stomach and prepare to march.

God, he's a sexy motherfucker. My mind immediately goes back to our make-out session in the car, and what do you know? I want a repeat so badly that my body starts to shake a little.

Wilma nudges my arm with her elbow and leans closer to whisper, "My nephew is a catch, isn't he? All the girls from his high school days fancied themselves in love with him. Broke a lot of hearts when he started dating that awful, selfish wench."

"We bumped into her last night," I say.

"You didn't! I reckon it wasn't a coincidence, was it?"

"No, I don't think so. I put the woman in her place, though."

My lips curl into a wicked grin and Wilma laughs softly. "Good for you. I always knew that dim-witted girl was bad news the moment Rori started dating her. My sixth sense never fails me, and it told me right away that she would cause great pain to my nephew. I wish I had been wrong."

"What does your sixth sense say about me?" I ask, too curious not to.

"Oh dear, you have nothing to worry about. You'll bring great joy to Rori, even if you don't believe it yet."

She walks away, leaving me with that little piece of vagueness. There are so many ways I can interpret her statement. My dirty mind immediately goes to the gutter, naturally. Visions of myself kneeling in front of him while I suck his cock assault me. My cheeks feel like lava, and when his little sister stops in front of me, my mortification increases tenfold. I bet my face is as red as Aunt Wilma's hair.

"Hi, I'm Lizzy, Rori's sister."

"I know. Nice to meet you, Lizzy," I smile, which she doesn't reciprocate.

"So, how you long have you been dating my brother? I've never heard of you until a few days ago, and there no pictures of you on his social media." The girl is looking at me with suspicion, and I don't know if I should be offended or amused. I guess if I was Rori's girlfriend for real, I'd probably be offended, but since I'm not, I'm leaning more toward the latter.

"A month or so."

"I checked you out. You like to party, huh?"

Okay, that comment ruffles my feathers. I won't tolerate that kind of judgmental tone from anyone, not even Rori's bratty little sister.

"You were spying on me?" I raise an eyebrow, but what I really want to do is glare.

She shrugs. "Of course. I have to look out for my brother. He's not very good when it comes to choosing his women."

"*Women*? How many are we talking about?"

"Er, I don't know. I suspect hundreds. So, you're not going to break his heart, are you?"

Hundreds. Right. That really sounds like Rori. *Not*. But again, I don't really know if he's not a Casanova. A couple weeks of minimal interaction don't make me an expert on him.

"I have no plans to do such a thing," I say. "But after hearing what you just told me, I think I'm the one who should be worried he'll break mine. Will he?" I cross my arms, narrowing my eyes.

"How am I supposed to know that? I don't have a crystal ball."

Suddenly Rori appears next to me, wrapping his arm around my waist. A delicious shiver runs down my spine at the same time my heart lurches forward. This won't do. I can't keep having these gut reactions every time he touches me. I'll end up combusting on the spot.

"Is my little sister giving you the third-degree already?"

"Oh no. We're just getting to know each other." I put on a phony smile.

"Right," he replies as if doesn't believe me. "Do you mind if I steal Emma for a few minutes, Lizzy?"

"Sure. I'll catch you later."

Rori lets go of my waist only to place his hand on my lower back and guide me toward the stairs. I don't ask where we're going because I have a hunch. The second floor is much quieter; we can hardly hear Rori's loud family down below. Once we reach the landing, Rori continues down the hallway until we're in front of the last door on the right. We go in, and I see our suitcases are already in the room, crammed next to a queen-size bed.

"I guess we're sleeping together, huh?" I say.

"I'm sorry. I tried to tell Mum about us, but—"

"Don't worry about it. I've resigned myself to play along with this charade for the week. I'll use it as practice for the future."

Rori doesn't reply to my statement; instead, he stares at me oddly. I shouldn't reciprocate, but here we are lost in each other's gazes, and I don't know what to make of it. My heart's pounding so fast, I'm afraid it's going to leap out of my chest. There's only one thought in my head: I want to kiss him again.

Rori breaks the connection first and turns to the bed. "I can sleep on the floor."

"Don't be silly. I think we can manage to share a bed. We'll put some pillows between ourselves. As long as you don't hog the bed, we'll be fine."

Rori looks at me like this is the worst idea in the world. It probably is, but this is like a game, and resisting Rori is the final battle I must face.

16

RORI

I try to give Emma space throughout the rest of the day, which isn't hard considering I have an entire family to use as a buffer. But I can't stop glancing at her from across the room from time to time. The excuse I give myself is that I'm only checking that she doesn't need rescuing, but fuck if that isn't complete horseshit. I can't stop looking at her for entirely different reasons. Her taste on my tongue is still there, sweet, intoxicating. The memory of how she felt in my arms is impossible to forget.

I hear her laugh and my eyes seek her out once more. My body reacts automatically, and I find myself rubbing away an ache in my chest.

"Rori, are you still with us, lad?" Uncle Paul snaps his finger in my face.

Reluctantly, I peel my gaze away from Emma and turn to him. He's smirking like he's just learned a secret he can't wait to share.

"Que pasa?" I ask.

My uncle chuckles and turns to Dad. "Que pasa. Is that Californian lingo?"

I shake my head. "I got it from Xavier, my bartender. Were you asking me something?"

He waves dismissively. "I forgot what I was saying already. But boy, you're smitten with that lass."

My spine goes taut in an instance as my defensive mechanism jumps into place. "It's not that bad."

"Not that bad." Uncle Paul nudges Dad with his elbow. "Did you hear that, Gerard?"

Dad watches me with an amused smirk and a glint of 'you're not fooling anyone' in his eyes.

"I can see the scarlet even from under that scruff on your face you call a beard," Uncle Paul continues.

My hand immediately goes to my face, as if rubbing it will make the blush go away. I had forgotten how impossible my uncle can be.

"Don't be embarrassed, son. As tough as we like to be, when we fall in love, we fall in love hard."

I open my mouth to deny I'm in love with Emma, but I can't bring myself to actually say the words.

Fuck me. Am I in love with Emma, the woman who claims she can't fall in love? What kind of glutton for punishment does that make me?

"The most important thing is that you're happy, Rori. Are you?"

My father's question is a loaded one, and it changes the mood of the conversation in an instant. The humor vanishes from my uncle's eyes, and the tension in my body has a different quality.

Swallowing hard, I nod. It doesn't seem to be good enough for Dad. His face twists into an expression of worry, so I'm quick to add a verbal answer.

"Yes, Dad. I'm happy."

At least, I haven't had a suicidal thought in years, but I don't say that bit out loud.

Mum comes into the living room and announces that dinner is ready. Glad for the interruption, I stand from the couch and am the first to head for the dining room. Like a lovesick puppy, I'm drawn to Emma immediately. She has a tray of food in her hand. It looks heavy, so I take it from her and set it on the table.

"Thanks, but I could handle that."

"It looked heavy," I say.

She narrows her eyes, pinching her lips at the same time. My eyes drop to her mouth as blood rushes through my veins. Fuck. I'm craving another taste of her, but she made it quite clear that there won't be a repeat of our make-out session.

Maybe it's wishful thinking in my part, but it seems she's not completely immune to my staring. Her jaw relaxes, and her mouth opens a little before her pink tongue makes an appearance as she licks her bottom lip. Stupid that I am, I reach out and rub my thumb over her lip, making her breath hitch.

"Don't do that," I say roughly.

"Do what?" She stares at my mouth as well, eyelids half open. I'm on the verge of doing something foolish, like kissing her again—and in front of my entire family to boot—when my sister Lizzy makes a gagging sound behind us.

"Get a room, will you?" She walks around the table and pulls out the chair right across from Emma. Probably to glare better at her.

Lizzy's used to being pampered by everyone, and also having my undivided attention when I come home. My guess is she's not enjoying sharing the spotlight with Emma.

The woman in question takes a step back and looks away. Her cheeks are flushed, which could be a sign of embarrassment and not desire. But I'm not a complete moron when it comes to reading body language. I know she wanted me to kiss her a second ago.

She sits and I follow her lead, trying to push thoughts of

Emma and her plump lips out of my head. Attraction or not, Emma has made up her mind. She doesn't want anything to do with me, and I will respect that.

For the first half hour, dinner goes smoothly, since everybody's more preoccupied with eating than giving us the third-degree. But I should've known the reprieve wouldn't last, and Lizzy is the one who begins the inquisition.

"So, Emma, what do you do for a living?"

"I was interning at an equity firm in New York, but I resigned."

"Why?" Lizzy watches Emma intently.

"Because I realized that wasn't what I wanted to do."

"So, you're a quitter." Lizzy leans back in her chair, smiling smugly.

"Elizabeth Marie O'Shea. What kind of manners is that?" Mum glares at my little sister from the other side of the table.

"What? I'm just calling it like it is."

"That's okay, Mrs. O'Shea," Emma cuts in. "No, Lizzy. I'm not a quitter. But I'm also not a doormat. I didn't see the point of sticking around a meaningless job with a terrible work atmosphere just for the sake of finishing something."

"That's easy for you to say when you're born rich," Lizzy grumbles.

"That's enough, Lizzy," I say before Mum can get up and drag away from the table. I know she's about to. Mum doesn't tolerate brattiness.

"No, that's okay, Rori. Being judged by the size of my inheritance is nothing new to me."

Shit, I'm 100 percent sure that barb was meant for me. I was that asshole who looked down on her, thinking she was another brainless, entitled rich girl. I think about that night she came into my pub, high as a kite, and how even despite my prejudice, she still beguiled me.

"I think it's bloody fantastic that you're rich. Somebody has to marry well in the family." Keira smirks in her fiancé's direction before taking a sip of her wine.

Clemmot puts a hand over his heart and twists his face into a grimace. "Ouch. You wound me, woman. I can't help it if the lottery gods haven't blessed me yet with the winning ticket."

"Yeah, yeah. Excuses, excuses." Keira stares straight into my eyes, pointing a fork in my direction. "Rori, you'd better not mess this up."

I mouth, "What the fuck?" to Keira before turning to Emma. I expect her to be mortified or annoyed, but she's chewing her food with a smirk on her lips. Then she turns, wiping her mouth with a napkin.

"What?"

"Don't listen to Keira. She's being obnoxious on purpose. Now you know why I live in California."

"Hmm, big mean Rori is running away from his sisters, huh?" Emma's eyes flash with mischief and what do you know, it gives a kick to my libido that has me straightening my jeans in the next moment.

"What was Rori like growing up? I want to know everything." She turns to the table again.

"A pain in my arse," Keira laughs. "He used to get into my stuff and steal my Barbies."

"Whoa, hold up." I raise both hands. "Before Emma starts to get the wrong idea, I didn't *steal* your Barbies, I borrowed them so my Action Man could save them."

"They always ended up naked. What the heck was your Action Man doing with them?"

A suppressed laugh comes from Emma's direction. She's covering her mouth, trying her best to rein her amusement in and doing a shoddy job at it.

"They were wearing the wrong clothes. Bloody dresses with frills and whatnot. I was trying to get them into more sensible clothes."

"Sure you were." Keira nods while her lips curve upward.

"Oh my, Rori. I didn't realize you were such a naughty little boy." Emma laughs out loud, and it's music to my ears. My irritation vanishes in an instant, replaced by a raw need to get closer to her.

Ignoring the warning bells in my head, I lean in and whisper in her ear. "You have no idea how naughty I can be."

There's a sharp intake of breath before she turns her face, bringing her lips dangerously close to mine.

"What are you doing, Rori?"

"I don't know."

"You're not going to kiss, are you?" Lizzy says, disgust lacing her question.

I pull back, forcing my facial expression back to neutral. No, there's no raging boner in my pants, nor is my heart galloping at full speed.

"Was Rori always a jock?" Emma asks.

Her questions is innocent, but she's unwittingly veered into a minefield. To disguise the sudden tension that descended on the room, I ask, "What makes you think I'm a jock?"

She rolls her eyes and puts her fork down. "Really, babe? You're going to make say it?"

I try to ignore how my heart reacts hearing the fake endearment, even it was dipped in sarcasm.

"Yes, sweetie, I'll make you say it."

Emma runs her fingers up my arms slowly, and I have to hold my breath before I lose my mind completely. She then wraps her hand around my bicep and squeezes. "You didn't get this by sitting on your butt."

"Maybe I just enjoy lifting weights."

"Rori was a football player. A damn good one, I might add," my father answers. I turn to him, not knowing what to expect. His head is down, focused on his plate of food.

"My knowledge of soccer goes as far as knowing which player looks better in their underwear. My vote is for David."

Keira raises her hand for a high five. "Preach, sista."

They're too far away to actually touch hands, so they settle for an air high five.

"No way, Ronaldo is way hotter," Lizzy chimes in.

Relieved that the topic has veered to who has the nicest ass, I lean back in my chair. But I'm far from relaxed. I don't know why Dad had to bring up my former glory days like that, as if I'd quit by choice. Of course, he only said I was a good player, which is true, but I know he thinks I'm a quitter. He was never on board with the idea of me spending time with his brother in California after what happened to me.

It's Emma's soft touch on my hand that brings me back to the here and now.

"Hey, is everything okay?"

"Yes, of course." I smile a little, but it's forced.

Her beautiful green eyes search my face, looking for clues. Emma's too smart to believe the lie. God, I want to kiss her so badly—among other things—that it physically hurts.

"You're not mad because I think David Beckham is sex on a stick, are you?"

I chuckle. "Of course not."

She moves closer, bringing her face a couple of inches from mine. For someone who doesn't want anything to do with me, she's doing a fine job of showing the contrary.

"You're sexier than him, so don't worry your pretty little head."

"Emma?"

"Yes."

"If you don't want me to kiss you again, you'd better stop saying shit like that."

She moves away as if being pulled by an invisible elastic band. "I'm sorry."

Things become tense between us after our exchange. Emma barely touches what's left of her food, and when she can make an escape, she claims her arm is bothering her and retires to her—*our*—room.

Fuck, how am I going to survive sleeping next to her?

There's only one thing that can help me, and that's getting so drunk that I'll get knocked down. So when Clemmot busts out a fine bottle of whiskey, I'm more than happy to raise my glass.

Here's to alcohol-induced oblivion.

17

EMMA

I'M A COWARD. THAT'S THE BRUTAL REALIZATION, AND MAYBE THE biggest takeaway from this trip. Rori's words are still reverberating in my brain as I lie in the small queen-size bed, staring at the ceiling. *"If you don't want me to kiss you again, you'd better stop saying shit like that."*

I'm not sure if my flirting is only a case of bad habit or if Rori's somehow snuck into my heart for real. All I know is that I want to be near him all the time, even when sex isn't on my mind. My heart twists painfully when the idea of him with other women enters my head. *Is this what falling in love feels like?*

With a huff, I turn on my side and immediately let out a low whimper. Shit, my arm. I had forgotten about it. I return to lying flat on my back, the most uncomfortable position to fall asleep in. I'm not the least bit tired, and the anticipation of Rori coming into my room is also not helping me relax. This is impossible.

I throw my legs to the side of the bed and sit up. Leaning forward, I fish out my iPad from the bag resting by the foot of the nightstand. If I can't sleep, I can at least catch up on my email. Half of the shit in my inbox is spam or newsletters I don't remember signing up for. One of these days, I'll have to go on a purge, but not tonight.

I click on an email from Dad. As usual, it's short and to the point. He hates his new diet, his doctor, and the fact that he's not allowed to return to his eighty-hours-a-week work schedule. He hopes I'm having a good time in Ireland and asks me to get shit-faced on St. Patrick's Day on his behalf since he can't.

I also have an email from Patricia, Dad's assistant, which in comparison to my father's reads like a novel. She's basically telling me the same stuff Dad did, but with way more details. Of course, Dad's being his difficult self. I should call him. He clearly needs a scolding, but I don't simply because I don't want to keep lying to him. I told him this was a work trip. If he knew my true intentions, he'd tell me I'm crazy, just like Rori did.

Ugh, and now we're back to Rori again.

Before I know what I'm doing, I'm on Facebook, looking through his profile. We're now friends there, so I have access to all his pictures, which sadly are only a handful. Because I'm obviously a glutton for punishment, I send a friend request to his friends, hoping to learn more about Rori's life.

Lewis accepts my request right away, and if I'm being completely honest with myself, his profile is the one I'm most interested in. I look through all his pictures, which is a task because the guy loves to take them. I suppose if you're a business owner, having a strong social media presence is important.

After scrolling through several, I finally find the one I'm looking for: Lewis and his cousin Alannah. Is it possible to develop hate at first sight, because I'm swimming in the ugly feeling right now. Trashy is the only word I can use to describe her. Again I wonder what the hell Rori saw in her.

She's tagged in the picture, so I pull up her profile. She's dumb enough not to have it set to private, which allows me to snoop all I want. My heartbeat increases as I begin to read her posts, hoping and dreading at the same time to find anything related to Rori. There's one at the top of her page from last night that can only refer to her encounter with Rori at the pub. **Fool me once, shame on you. Fool me twice, shame on me.** *Is she serious? She was the one who dumped Rori, and she's blaming him for that? What else does she have to say about him?* They've been broken up for almost a decade, so there's little chance she'll have anything on her page still from that time. But like a junkie looking for his next fix, I keep searching.

Five minutes later, I'm staring a picture of a teen Rori. His hair is short, his face devoid of any scruff. He has Alannah in his arms and she's holding a bouquet of flowers. They're both dressed in formal wear, but it's the happiness on their faces that makes my stomach bottom out. The caption says **First task on the Alannah & Rori Forever plan accomplished. Bride's bouquet caught.** I can't help but read the comments, and the first one is from Rori. **LOL. I guess I should start looking for that ring, then.**

Oh my God. He was serious about that chick. Miles wasn't kidding.

I don't know what I should do, keep reading their convo or just shut the damn iPad off. In the end, I choose the latter. I'm suffering from my major retroactive jealousy, and it's doing my head in.

I flop back on the bed, my head hitting the pillow with a muffled thud. I can't keep playing this cat-and-mouse game with Rori. I have to know if what I'm feeling is only sexual frustration or if there's more.

Rori

I know I've drunk enough when I can barely make it up the stairs without tripping and falling flat on my face. Things don't improve when I reach the landing. The floor seems to be moving, and I have to hold onto the walls to be able to walk a semi-straight line. Drinking almost an entire bottle of single malt whiskey will do that to you. The hangover tomorrow will be a beast.

In front of the bedroom door, I stop for a moment with my hand already on the knob. My heart's pounding in my chest despite the drunken stupor. It's past two in the morning, so Emma should be sound asleep. One can only hope. If she's awake and says anything remotely close to what she said at dinner, I won't be able to restrain myself.

Shit. Getting drunk might not have been the smartest idea after all.

I push the door open, wincing as it creaks loudly. The room is shrouded in darkness besides the soft glow coming from an object next to Emma—her iPad is my guess. Walking on tiptoes, I approach the bed and pull the device away. She moans in her sleep right before turning on her back. I stay frozen to the spot, hovering over her sleeping form like a creep.

She continues to talk in her sleep. At first it's a bunch of incoherent mumbo jumbo, until the name Declan escapes her lips. I recoil, the sound of that name spoken while she's in dreamland feeling like a lash across my face. I pivot, ready to get the hell out of the room. Maybe I can sleep in my father's office.

"Rori, please don't leave me. I'm so afraid." Emma's voice is low but filled with panic.

I turn, thinking she's awake. She's not. Her eyes are still closed, and her eyebrows seem to be knitted together. She begins to shake her head from side to side while a soft cry leaves her throat. She's having a nightmare.

Faster than a speeding train, I sit next to her and pull her head onto my lap.

"Emma, sweetheart. Wake up." I run my fingers through her hair.

She turns her face, burrowing her nose into my crotch. My dick springs to life, even though this is the most inappropriate moment for an erection. I push her away gently, and suddenly her eyes fly open.

"Rori?"

"Yes, it's me."

"What time is it?"

"A little over two. Are you okay?"

Emma scooches away a little and rubs her eyes. "Yes. Just the usual garden-variety nightmare."

"Do you want to talk about it? You sounded a little distressed."

With a shaky breath, she sits up and then brings her knees to her chest. "I was dreaming about Brussels." She wraps her good arm around her legs and rests her cheek on her knees, her face toward me.

"You said my name." The words leave my lips before I can stop them. If I'd been sober, it wouldn't have happened.

"I did?" She raises her head. "Just your name?"

"You asked me not to leave you. I guess you probably meant Declan." *No, I don't sound bitter at all.*

She keeps staring at me for the longest time without saying a word. Then she extends her arm. "Come here."

Like a fool, I don't hesitate, don't pause to think, just take her offered hand and sit closer. My palm is on her cheek and I don't have the slightest idea how it ended up there. I don't recall making the decision to put it there. My brain's fuzzy as hell, and maybe this isn't even real. Maybe I'm passed out somewhere and this is just a dream.

She leans closer, reaching over and pulling at the elastic band securing the bun on top of my head. My hair falls loose like a waterfall and frames my face. She runs her fingers through it, and it's so fucking good, I close my eyes to savor it.

I'm definitely dreaming.

"Rori?"

"Hmm?"

"Kiss me?"

My eyes fly open, my sight now adjusted to the darkness. She's waiting for my answer with lips partially open and eyes trained on my mouth. I should ask her if she's sure, but my good judgment drowned in the third glass of whiskey I had tonight. I pull her to me without a second thought, claiming her mouth as if I'm a starving man and her kisses are the only sustenance I need.

If this isn't a dream, I'm definitely going to Hell.

18

EMMA

"Kɪss me?" I'm not asking, I'm begging.

My chest feels tight, not because of the nightmare but because I couldn't find Rori in the confusion. I don't know why my mind placed him in that scene; all the other times the nightmare assaulted me, I'd been alone. This time he was there, and I was terrified of losing him. Now that I'm wide awake, the fear still lingers.

The palm on my cheek moves to the back of my head, Rori's fingers tangling in my hair before he pulls me to him and covers my mouth with his for a hard, dirty, earth-shattering kiss. I can taste the whiskey on his tongue; he's clearly been drinking a lot, but he's far from sloppy. On the contrary, Rori takes possession of my mouth with the precision of an expert lover, and I want his tongue all over my body, even my jagged scar—which should terrify me, but it doesn't.

With an impatient hand, I grab the back of his sweater and pull it up. Rori leans back, his breathing all out of whack, and finishes what I started, removing not only the sweater but also the T-shirt underneath. My eyes drop to his wide chest, smooth and hard. It rises and falls fast, as if Rori's just run a marathon.

A simple silver cross hangs from a thin chain around his neck. I trace the accessory with the tips of my fingers before moving the caress to his warm skin. Unable to contain myself, I lean over and kiss his chest, right where his heart is.

"Emma, I've been drinking," he says, his voice rough and restrained.

I bring my eyes back to his face. "If you don't want me to touch you, I can stop."

He grabs my hand, bringing it to his lips, and kisses the tip of my fingers. A zing of pleasure shoots down straight to my core.

"That's the problem," he says. "I don't want you to stop. On the contrary, I want you. *All* of you."

I lie back down and raise my hand to him. "Then have me."

"Are you sure?"

"Yes," I breathe out, then grab his hand and place it between my legs. "Can you feel how much I want you?"

Rori leans forward, hovering over me now, and takes over. His body's still poised above mine without touching, but he's doing just fine with his hand. He applies pressure to my core, and the friction of the fabric of my pajama pants against my clit makes my eyes roll back into their sockets. I moan out loud because it feels so good.

"Do you like that?"

"Yes," I hiss. "I want more."

"Me too."

He pulls my pants down, and I'm panting heavily by the time he lobs them to a corner of the room. He kept my panties on, though I don't know what for. It seems he's going out of his way to torture me.

"Rori, I need you to touch me."

"Patience, my dear."

He traces my belly with a featherlight touch, going lower and lower until he finds the edge of my panties. My breath hitches when he slides his index finger underneath the lace, moving it back and forth, a sensuous tease so close to where I want it to be. My fingers curl around the sheets as my back arches forward.

"God, you're so wet already. I need a taste." He pulls his finger back, bringing it to his mouth to suck my juices off it. I might come just from watching him.

"Fucking delicious," he says. "I want more."

All coherent thought hops onto a magical carpet and takes off when Rori rubs his nose against my panties before sucking the delicate fabric into his mouth.

"Oh God. I'm going to come," I say.

"Hold on a little longer, Em. I need to feel your orgasm on my tongue." He pushes my panties to the side, and with a long, languid stroke of his tongue brings me to the edge of ultimate bliss. There's no holding back. I come strong and hard as Rori sucks my clit into his mouth. I have to put a pillow over my face to muffle my cries. That was the fastest orgasm I've ever had in my life.

Rori keeps licking and sucking until the tremors racking my body cease. I push the pillow off my face and my hands tangle in his hair. With a soft yank—I'm loving his Tarzan tresses—I urge him up my body so I can kiss him again. He stops before I can bring his mouth to mine, making me frown.

"What's wrong?"

"I'm about to come in my jeans, but I want this to be fair."

He sits on the balls of his feet and grabs the edge of my top. Panicking, I wrap my fingers around his wrists, stopping him. "I always keep my top on."

"You don't need to hide from me, Em. Your body is lovely, scar and all, and I want to worship it properly."

When I still won't let go of his writs, he adds, "Please? I'm begging you."

"What did you say?' I whisper, my hold on him slacking.

He leans closer, stopping an inch away from my mouth. "I. Am. Begging. You."

Just like in the dream. *Oh my God, was that a premonition?* No, that's absurd, but how come those words out of his mouth give me a sense of déjà vu? I drop my hands, letting Rori do whatever he wants. He pulls the fabric up inch by inch, kissing my belly as he goes. Goose bumps form on my arms, and I rub my legs together to get rid of the sudden ache between them. I'm so not satiated yet.

When Rori kisses the beginning of my scar, I tense.

"It's okay, Em. You don't have to feel self-conscious with me. You. Are. Beautiful." He punctuates each word with a kiss. When it comes to getting it off my arm, Rori does so with all the care in the world. The muscle's still a little tender, but it's easy to forget the pain when it's followed by another smoldering kiss. His arms go around my back, and with deft fingers, he unhooks my bra. My boobs break free, but Rori doesn't immediately divert his attention to them. He continues devoting his time to my lips while he grazes the underside of my breasts with the softest of touches.

I moan against his mouth, unable to keep the sound bottled in. Rori chuckles right before he cups my tits, squeezing them softly and then pinching my nipples. My fingers find his hair which, serves as the cue for him to explore the rest of my body with his tongue. He leaves a trail of hot kisses as he goes down my neck, then my collarbone, finally arriving at the swell of my breasts. He licks one of my nipples as if I was an ice cream cone before latching onto it and drawing it into his mouth. I'm ready to straddle him when he pushes me back gently, shifting his body as he suckles so he's stretching out on top of me, falling in between my legs.

His erection presses against my core through the jeans he's still wearing. His hips pump into me, mimicking what's to come, and out of nowhere a bout of nervousness hits me. My body begins to shake, so to disguise the odd reaction, I let my hands explore Rori's backside. I stop when I find the seam of his jeans, and then I break the kiss to complain.

"I thought you wanted to make things fair. This"—I squeeze his butt through the jeans—"isn't fair."

"All right, you win." He rolls off me and jumps out of the bed.

I lean on my elbow to better ogle the man. With all that hair, unbound and wide, he's an Irish Tarzan and I'm about become his Jane. This is not a simple hookup; I know it deep in my bones. Such certainty should have me out the door like the Flash, but the panic, the urge to flee isn't there, at least not right now.

He pulls his pants down, boxer shorts and all, and holy Mary mother of God, his cock must be the reference they use to make dildos, because it's the most beautiful thing I've ever seen. And that's saying a lot, because dicks are not the most attractive part of the human body. But Rori's is pure perfection. My mouth begins to water, and I can't wait to have that piece of equipment between my legs.

"I have to warn you. There's almost an entire bottle of whiskey running through my veins, so I might not perform as well as I want to."

I tap the mattress. "Lie down here, boy, and let me take care of the rest."

Rori's lips twists into a smile as he does what I asked. As soon as he's lying by my side, he reaches for me, his hand cupping my face at the same time his lips cover mine. I sense he wants to roll on top of me, but I have other ideas. I bite his lower lip, pulling slightly before breaking the connection. With my hand flat against his chest, I push him back a little.

"Down, boy. I'm running the show."

I roll him onto his back, straddling him at the same time. Belatedly, I remember that I'm still wearing my underwear, and that we're missing a condom. I'm done with foreplay, so I hop off him. Now it's my turn for a quick stripping session. Rori watches me remove my panties with hooded eyes, and the fact that I—with ugly scar on full display and all—can get him to look at me like that is the best compliment he could give me.

I throw my underwear to the side and stand completely naked in front of him. I haven't done this since the accident, and even in the dark room, I'm a little unnerved to be so exposed. My arm twitches as I automatically want to cover the scar, but I fight the involuntarily reaction.

"Not that I'm not appreciating the view, but I'd prefer it if you came back to bed," Rori protests.

Without taking my eyes off him, I grab the toiletries pouch from inside my purse on the floor and fish out a condom. Then I return to bed, positioning myself by his legs to slowly crawl up the length of his body. Rori's breathing becomes more labored the closer I get to my goal. Curling my fingers around his rock-hard erection, I rub my thumb over the head, trailing precum over the soft skin. Rori makes a sound in the back of his throat that's all male.

"Lass, you're killing me."

"I was never called lass before. Say it again." I move my hand up and down his shaft.

"Lass... fuck, this feels good."

"It's about to get better." I run my tongue over the length of his dick until I reach the top.

Rori twitches under my ministrations, and when I bring his erection into my mouth, his hips buck. He clearly wants to take control of the situation, but I'm having none of that. It's my turn to have some fun.

He's so big, I can barely fit his girth into my mouth, but I give it my all, bringing his head all the way to the back of my throat before slowly pulling back as I suck hard.

"Em, I don't think I'll last long like that, so forgive me for this."

In a ninja move, Rori grabs me by my shoulders and rolls me over. I let out a yelp that's muffled when his mouth covers mine. Leaning on his forearms, he keeps his upper body off me, probably so he doesn't squish my arm. It's throbbing a little more thanks to his impulsive maneuver, but the feel of his cock teasing at my entrance overrides any pain.

"Condom," I say before the delicious sensation down below overrides common sense as well.

Breaking the kiss, he takes the foil packet from my hand and rips it open. When the rubber stretches down his length, I'm afraid it'll break. I'll have to buy extra-large next time.

The old Emma wouldn't even think about a next time. No, I'd be plotting my exit strategy already, but with Rori I want many, many next times. A sliver of fear lodges itself in my heart, but when he kisses me again and his cock slides into my hot sheath slowly, the unwelcomed feeling vanishes.

I bring him down on me, ignoring my limp arm across my belly. I want to feel the entire length of his body against mine. I want to be claimed through and through. His kiss deepens as he pulls out almost completely to ram back into me with a powerful stroke.

And I'm gone, gone, gone.

19

EMMA

THE LIGHT STREAMING THROUGH THE GAP IN THE CURTAINS WAKES me from one of the most peaceful sleeps I've had in ages. The ache between my legs and the tingling on my lips tell me that what happened last night wasn't a dream. Rori and I finally succumbed to the undeniable chemistry between us, and I'm kicking myself for being so stubborn and not giving in sooner.

I reach behind me but find that side of the bed empty and cold. I roll over, wanting to see for myself that Rori isn't in bed with me. Nope, I'm definitely alone. After last night, I expected to wake up in his arms, and maybe have an encore. Disappointment makes my chest tight and I rub my sternum, trying to ease the pain. Maybe I overslept.

I reach for my phone on the nightstand and see it's still early, not even nine yet. *Okay, Emma. Don't freak out. Maybe Rori's just an early riser.* I move quickly, throwing my legs to the side of the bed and standing up. A quick shower is in order before I show my face downstairs.

Ten minutes later, I make my way down to the living room, heart stuck in my throat. I hear Rori's voice coming from the kitchen, and the jitters in my belly increase by a million. But I stop short when his words become discernible and the name Declan reaches my ear.

What the actual fuck.

I make my presence known, entering the kitchen with a fake smile plastered on my face. I'm greeted by an audience of solemn faces—his parents, his sisters, even his uncle and aunt. My smile wilts like a flower in the dead of the winter. I turn to Rori with a question in my gaze and the feeling of betrayal in my heart.

"You told them?"

Rori's standing, leaning against the kitchen counter with his arms crossed. He nods once, clenching his jaw hard.

"Everything?" My voice comes out like a shrill while my arm goes around my middle. *Why, Rori? Why?*

His mother stands and pulls me into her arms, hugging me as tight as the sling will allow. "Don't be mad at Rori, honey. He didn't want to tell us. He only asked if we knew a Declan Kelly. It was our need to know everything that forced his hand."

Aunt Wilma stands by my side and demands a hug as well. "You poor thing. I can't imagine going through a nightmare like that."

At this point, I'm just going through the motions like a puppet. I'm stunned. I can't believe Rori jumped the gun like that before talking to me first. There's only one explanation for his behavior—he regrets what happened between us last night. Isn't that ironic. The first time I'm willing to take a chance on someone, to jump off the edge, and he doesn't want me.

My throat feels tight and my eyes sting. Fucking Rori is going to make me cry.

With a sniffle, I take a step back and glance away, wiping a rogue tear from the corner of my eye. I'm sure the gesture wasn't lost on anyone, but at least they won't know the real reason why I'm crying.

"I think there was a Kelly in my year at school," Keira says.

"Though his first name was Martin, not Declan. Martin D. Kelly, actually, so maybe Declan was his middle name. What does he look like, Emma?"

"Hmm, tall, dark brown hair, blue eyes, I think. I'm sorry, I know it's not a very good description."

"Considering how you met this guy, it's a miracle you remember all that," Aunt Wilma chimes in.

"I wish my stuff wasn't all in storage already. We could look at my yearbook," Keira muses.

"Doesn't Rori have one too?" Lizzy asks.

"It's probably gone," he replies roughly, standing a little straighter.

"No, no, I put your things away in the attic." His mother turns to her husband. "Gerard, do you think you can help me find that box?"

"Of course, of course." The man stands up, throwing a pained look in Rori's direction. I'm too overwhelmed with the sudden development to dwell too much on that exchange.

Rori turns to me then, his face still an unreadable mask. The shock begins to dissipate, and fury takes its place. The last thing I want is to blow a fuse in front of his family, though.

"I think I need some fresh air."

"Rori, why don't you take Emma for a tour of the farm?" his mom suggests.

Fuck, I don't want to spend time alone with him. The idea clearly displeases him as well, if the frown on his forehead is any indication.

"I thought I could help Dad in the attic. There may be a few things I'd like to bring back with me to California," he says.

"I can take you on a tour," Lizzy offers. "Do you know how to ride a horse?"

"Oh, Lizzy. Emma can't ride a horse with her arm in a sling like that," her mom says.

I haven't ridden a horse in ages, so the idea sounds absolutely fantastic to me, bum arm or not.

"I'm an expert equestrian. I used to compete when I was younger and won several first prize trophies. I can manage riding with only one arm."

"Is that so?" Rori's mom looks out the window and sighs. "The weatherman predicted rain today, but I think you'll be good for a couple of hours."

"Don't worry, Mum. Besides, a little rain never killed anyone."

The teen walks out of the kitchen, and it's clear she expects me to follow her. I have a moment of weakness, throwing a glance in Rori's direction. He's staring down at his shoes and doesn't sense my stare. Or maybe he does and he's avoiding it.

My ego is bruised, no doubt, but the ache in my chest is due to something else. A bruised heart.

And here it is, the truth I knew all along. Love is for fools. I should never have made that promise to Dad. The notion that there's one person in the entire universe made especially for you is bogus. It's the biggest lie ever told. But people buy that shit over and over again; the billion-dollar wedding industry is there to prove it.

I walk out the front door and see Lizzy turn a corner ahead. Gee, would it kill for her to wait up? The stable's behind the main house, just a short distance walking. I don't know why she offered to give me a tour if she didn't want to. It seems assholery is a family trait.

The sharp smell of manure reaches my nose before we even cross into the stable. It's a rather small space with only six stalls, two of which are empty. Lizzy opens the gate of the first one to her right. Speaking softly, she pats the mane of a middle-size mare.

"Hello, Margaret. Are you ready for a ride?"

The horse lifts her head and whinnies as if saying yes. Lizzy coaxes the horse out, and without a glance in my direction, she begins to saddle the animal. "Margaret is old, but she's the easiest horse we have. She's great with children, so it'll be perfect for you."

I don't miss the jab, and I'm not one to take punches without firing back. "Because of my arm? I'm a champion of show jumping. I can manage a horse with more personality."

"Show jumping, huh?" Lizzy gives me a haughty look. "Then you should definitely ride Thunder. I'm usually the only one who can ride him, but since you're an expert."

The little brat is challenging me. We'll see who has the last laugh.

She opens the last stall, revealing a black, tall stallion. He's not a purebred, but he's a beautiful animal nonetheless. He whinnies affectionately when Lizzy pats his nose. "This one is a firecracker, just like his father was. I miss Storm, but I also hate him."

"Why? What happened to him?"

She turns to me, her big green eyes wide in surprise. "You don't know?"

"Uh, no? Should I?"

Lizzy lets out a heavy sigh and glances away. "He's the reason Rori left us."

"I don't follow. He moved to California because of a horse?"

"Rori was a football star. He had scouts coming from all over the country to try to recruit him. He was the town's pride and joy, and everyone adored him. Then he took Storm out for a last ride before he was set to visit a football club that wanted to sign him. And then everything changed."

Lizzy pauses as if the memory is too painful to relieve. Rori moved to California when he was eighteen, if I'm not mistaken, so she must've been only seven years old.

"What changed?" I whisper, afraid to know the answer.

She turns to me with eyes brighter than before. "Lightning

struck a tree near Rori. The loud noise spooked Storm and he went mad, took off. Rori couldn't control him. The horse twisted one of his front ankles, and during the fall, Rori's right leg got pinned under Storm. He broke it in three different spots. I'm surprised you haven't noticed the scars."

Guilt makes my cheeks burn like lava. It was too dark in the room last night, and my attention was diverted to another part of his body.

"Of course I did. But as the bearer of my own ugly scar—" I pause and lift my sweater, showing Lizzy the jagged red line that adorns my torso. "—I didn't ask Rori about his."

I can't believe I'm doing this. I've never shown my scar so casually before, especially to a person I barely know. Maybe fucking Rori last night without my top on changed how I feel about it. Lizzy's jaw slackens, and maybe I'm imagining things, but when she raises her eyes to mine, I don't read contempt in them anymore.

"That looks worse than his," she finally says. "I'd never be able to take my clothes off in front of anyone if I had such an ugly scar."

I wince despite my attempt to not let Lizzy get to me. "I used to feel like that, but now I don't give a fuck."

"I'm sorry. I didn't mean to make you feel bad."

Holy shit. Did she just apologize? She does look remorseful.

I wave it away. "Don't stress over it. I have thick skin. Now, how about we take these horses out before the weather turns?"

20

RORI

WHEN MY FATHER CALLED ME INTO HIS OFFICE, I HAD NO IDEA what he wanted to talk about. I thought were going to the attic to look for my old yearbook, which was not a task I was looking forward to. It was the quickest excuse I could find to avoid playing guide to Emma, though. I knew she didn't want my company; I could read it in her glacial stare.

The reality of the huge mistake I made last night crashed into me when I woke up this morning with her in my arms. She felt so good curled against my chest, but I was certain she wouldn't feel the same. I took advantage of her in a moment of vulnerability. She had just woken up from a nightmare. The drunk fool I was couldn't say no when she asked for a kiss, but I should've known better. I should've stopped.

So I tried to make amends by asking my family about Declan. Unfortunately, they're all too fucking curious for their own good and wouldn't stop pestering me about why Emma was looking for the man. The hangover mixed with my frustration, and I ended up making another mistake and telling them about Brussels, something that was clearly a betrayal to

Emma's trust. It seems that when it comes to that woman, I can't get my shit straight.

Dad's behind his desk, so I force my head back into the here and now. I can obsess about Emma later. He and I used to be closer when I was younger—or more precisely, before my accident. He was my biggest cheerleader, taking me to football practice every Sunday, going to all my games. He used to play football when he was younger too, but he always told me he'd never been as good as me. From a young age, I've always wanted to impress the guy. He was my hero, after all. So when shit happened, the biggest blow wasn't losing my brilliant football career, it was disappointing him.

I sit in stunned silence across from him after he tells me the reason for this private conversation. The bed-and-breakfast is in deep trouble. Dad made some bad investments, and in consequence, had to take out a second mortgage on the property. Top that with below expectations reservations and he's on the verge of losing everything if he can't come up with the money to pay the bank.

"Dad, I'm really sorry to hear that."

"I know. I haven't told your mother yet, and I'm terrified to do so."

"I wish I had the money. I'd give it to you in a heartbeat."

His back meets the chair's padding behind him as he frowns. "I didn't tell you expecting a handout, Rori. I was hoping you could give me some fresh ideas in marketing. I still have some time until payment's due."

"Yeah, I can help you with that for sure. But Dad, why are you putting up with the family here during the busiest week of the season? You could be making a killing."

"Your sister wanted to get married this week, and well, I couldn't ask our relatives to stay at a hotel in town. That wouldn't be right."

I shake my head. This is probably the reason Dad's in trouble, no doubt. It shows a lack of business sense. He should've told Keira to postpone the wedding at least a week. I don't see the hurry.

There are so many things I'd like to say on the matter, but it's too late now. I ask Dad to show me everything he's done so far in terms of marketing, and together we start to formulate a plan. I don't know how long we spend locked in the office—at least an hour, I think—when suddenly the door bursts open and in comes Lizzy, wetter than a drowned rat.

"What's the matter, child?" Dad stares at Lizzy wide-eyed.

She locks gazes with me. "I lost Emma."

I stand, my body coiled with tension. "What do you mean you lost Emma?"

Lizzy shakes her head, and I think she's on the verge of crying. "I-I don't know. We took the horses out, and I stopped for a few minutes to take a call and she vanished."

I close my eyes for a split second and pinch the bridge of my nose. I should've never allowed her to go out on a horse, especially with one of her arms incapacitated. I'm such a moron.

"What horse is she riding, Lizzy?" Dad asks.

Guilt shines in my sister's eyes before she drops her gaze to the floor. "Thunder."

I whip my face to Dad. "Isn't that Storm's spawn?"

"Yes," he replies, then clenches his jaw tight.

For fuck's sake. That horse is just as bad as his father was. I want to yell at Lizzy for allowing Emma to ride him, but I can't place all the guilt on her shoulders. I'm the one who fucked everything up.

I storm out of Dad's office and head toward the stables. The sky's opened in fat, cold droplets of water. It's raining so hard it's impossible to see out in the distance. Lizzy follows me into the stables, hugging herself as she tries to control her shivering.

"Get back inside before you catch a cold."

"What are you going to do?"

"What do you think? I'm going after her."

"But you haven't ridden a horse since the accident."

"I'll be fine." I saddle a brown horse. I'm not sure what it's called. "Where did you lose her?"

"Near the river, by the horseshoe bend."

I pull my cell phone out, hoping to reach Emma, but Lizzy tells me she had nothing on her.

"Great. Okay, she can't have gone too far. Now get back in the house."

Propping my left foot in the stirrup, I swing my right leg over the horse's back, getting onto the saddle with ease. I guess it's the same as riding a bike. My hands curl around the leather rein as I get a flash of the pivotal moment that changed my life forever. My adrenaline levels spike and my heart decides now's a good time to go on a sprint. I focus on my breathing, trying to calm the fuck down. I'll be of no use to Emma if I lose control, if I let my emotions take over.

I can do this. Emma needs me. Thinking about her helps me get centered again, and with a tap of my feet against the horse's flank, I command him to spring forward.

Cold rain pelts against my skin, the drops feeling like ice shards instead of water. The place where Lizzy last saw Emma isn't far, only a couple of minutes from the house, but I don't see it until I'm almost upon it. There's no sign of Emma, so I keep galloping until I approach an area where the trees are more abundant. I veer for the forest, slowing the horse to a trot, not wanting to risk the animal tripping over an exposed tree root. The trees offer some cover against the rain, and I hope that was Emma's thinking. There's also an old cabin in the woods, so there's hope she found it.

I follow the man-made track of beaten ground which has turned into mud. The cabin comes into view after a few minutes, and relief runs through me when I see Thunder out front, tied to a tree. I call out her name, my voice booming into the silent forest.

"Rori? I'm over here."

She walks out of the cabin, her blonde hair drenched and pasted to her face, her clothes molded to her body. I increase my pace, stopping only when I'm a few inches from her. She's paler than usual, and her lips are almost blue. Offering my jacket won't do any good since it's also soaking wet, so I pull her into my arms.

"You're freezing."

"I know. I'm a human popsicle."

Her good arm sneaks around my waist and I pull her closer, not wanting to let her go. My heart's racing once more, but for completely different reasons. I pull back, capturing Emma's cold face between my hands. "Are you okay? What happened?"

"I got carried away and didn't notice Lizzy wasn't behind me until too late. Then the rain started and I couldn't see a foot in front of me, so I decided to wait here."

A sensible plan if she weren't soaked to the bone. But I don't say that to her, not when I want to do other things besides scolding her. Memories of last night come to the forefront of my mind and in a moment, all I can hear is the sound of my pulse rushing in my ears. I run my thumb against her lips, unable to stop myself, but Emma doesn't flinch, just stares into my eyes.

"Your lips are ice-cold," I whisper.

"They feel ice-cold." She inches closer, and I find myself doing the same. "Rori?"

"Yes, Emma."

"Why did you leave me this morning?" Her question catches me completely off-guard, as does the vulnerable glint in her eyes.

"I thought it would make things easier for you."

"What? Why would you think that?"

"I took advantage of you, Em. I'm so, so sorry."

Her delicate eyebrows furrow together right before she steps back and out of my embrace. "I asked you to kiss me. How does that equal to you taking advantage of me?"

"You had just woken up from a nightmare. You were vulnerable."

Emma laughs, but it's devoid of any humor. "That's the stupidest thing I've ever heard." She marches in my direction and pokes the middle of my chest. "I'm not a damsel in distress who needs to be saved at every turn. Nor am I a dim-witted bimbo who needs a man to do the thinking for me. I can make my own damn decisions, and if I asked you to kiss me last night, it didn't stem from vulnerability. I wanted your lips on mine, I wanted your cock between my legs. And honestly, I wanted to do it all over again this morning, only you weren't there."

I grab her hand so she'll stop poking me. "What are you saying, Emma? Do you want to use me until you find your precious Declan, is that it?"

Her eyebrows shoot up to the heavens as her lips make a tiny O. The fire dims in her gaze before she pulls her hand back. "I-I don't know what I want."

That should be my answer to leave things alone. I should walk away from her, but I do the exact opposite. I grab her face again and kiss her without mercy, without a second thought. It's raw, demanding, and it mirrors every single contradicting emotion swirling in my chest. There's no resistance on her part; she surrenders willing to the invasion.

Letting go of her face, I cup the back of her head, my fingers tangling with her hair. There's no containing what's happening between us, and before I know it, I have Emma's leg wrapped around my waist and I'm walking inside the cabin. This is really just a place to take a rest, so there's nothing in terms of furniture besides a wooden table and a couple of chairs. I ignore them for now and push Emma against the wall. My hips pump against hers and my cock complains that the friction, despite being fucking amazing, isn't enough. I want to bury myself deep in her hot sheath again.

I pivot and place Emma on the table. She knows exactly what's on my mind when she reaches for my fly. Her jeans are harder to get out of the way, though. The wet fabric is stubbornly clinging to her skin, and it takes forever to peel them off.

"Bloody hell. Why must you wear these skintight things?"

She laughs. "Because they make my ass look good."

I kiss the side of her mouth. "Lass, you'll look good in anything, but I prefer you like this, naked and wet for me."

Emma tangles her hand in my hair and yanks me back to her lips. "Shut up and kiss me properly."

I'm more than happy to comply while my hand gets busy with her sweet pussy. I apply pressure on her clit with my thumb, making lazy circles, and loving the little moaning sounds coming from the back of Emma's throat. My fingers are slick from her juices, so it makes it really easy to insert my forefinger in her heat.

"Oh my God, Rori. What are you doing to me?"

"Getting you warm?"

"I need you inside."

"I am inside." I chuckle.

She hits my arm. "Don't be a smartass. Do you want me to spell it out?"

"Yes, Emma. I'd love it if you told me exactly what's on your mind."

"Fine. I want your big, swollen cock inside of me. Happy now?"

I let out a groan before I kiss her again, increasing the tempo of my finger pumping into her pussy. She allows me that for a few seconds before she gets impatient and pulls away.

"Do you have a condom?"

Without answering, I pull my wallet from my back pocket

and fish out the little foil packet. "Always be prepared is my motto."

"Prepared or forever hopeful?" Emma eyes twinkle when she laughs, and my heart feels a little heavy all of a sudden. I ignore the feeling and focus on the now. She's here, watching me from hooded eyes, laughing at my words. There's no sense worrying about the future.

I toss the condom's packaging to the floor and get ready as fast as I can. Emma yanks me toward her when I'm done, opening herself to me and wrapping her legs behind my ass. Holding her waist to keep her in place, I plunge in and we both groan at the same time. She feels even better now that my thoughts aren't clouded by alcohol. I don't know what's better, her pussy creaming around my cock or her tongue tangling with mine.

She throws her head back when the orgasm washes over her, screaming at the top of her lungs, unafraid that someone might hear her. Watching her shatter like that only pushes me over the edge, and now I'm the one yelling as my seed spills free. My body convulses as the last vestiges of climax are released. I hide my face in the crook of her neck and breathe in her sweet scent. My heart's beating at warp speed, and there's a rushing in my ears. This isn't a simple fuck—it's way more than that, at least to me.

Once my breath returns to normal, I pull away, careful to keep the condom in place. Emma's face is bright red, and her eyes watch me with a glint of desire.

"What are you thinking?" I ask.

"I'm thinking that I wish I wasn't freaking cold, but I could do this again, right here."

I smile. "Me too, lass." I bend over and pick up her jeans, not knowing how she'll manage to get back in them.

I give her the piece of clothing almost apologetically.

"Ugh, how terrible would it be if I didn't put them back on? They're not going to keep me warm."

"If you don't mind showing up at the house with your arse hanging." I shrug.

She looks at the jeans, then at me. "No, I actually don't mind."

Emma slides off the table and puts her panties on. Then she bends over to grab her boots when she stops suddenly. "What's this?"

She unfurls from her crouch slowly and then turns to me, holding the empty condom foil. I narrow my eyes, not knowing what her question's about, when I recognize the logo on it. *Fuck, fuck, fuck.* I used the custom condom I bought from her when she came over to my pub. Idiot that I am, I kept one in my wallet for I don't know what reason.

"Rori, why do you have one of Peyton's bachelorette party favors in your wallet?"

I rub my face to buy time, but there's no way of answering that without telling Emma the truth about how we met.

"You sold it to me."

"What?"

"You came into the pub the night of the bachelorette party and sold it to me as part of a dare."

Emma blinks at me several times before her eyes widen. She covers her mouth with her hand and takes a step back.

"No," she whispers, eyes wide.

21

———

EMMA

IT TAKES ME A MOMENT BUT THEN, ONCE THE FINAL PIECE OF THE puzzle clicks in my head, it's like a vault's been unlocked and my memories from that wild night burst through. I remember going into Rori's pub, seeing him for the first time and going weak at the knees. I called dibs on him so none of my friends could flirt with him. Then I tried to sell condoms to the guy. The part when I returned to the pub without my friends is a little fuzzier, but I recall enough.

"You took me home that night," I say.

"Yes."

"And I tried to seduce you."

He nods.

Shame takes over me. Rori said no and I threw a tantrum. No wonder he thought I was bad news when I returned months later, looking like I was coming from another night of debauchery.

"Why didn't you tell me?" I ask.

"I didn't think you'd ever remember, and I didn't want to upset you." He takes a step forward. "Come on, Em. Don't be that way."

Ignoring his outstretched hand, I walk around him and out of the cabin. The rain's stopped, but the cold is just as bad or worse now that I'm pantsless. I untie Thunder and prepare to mount him when Rori grabs my wrist. "Why don't you take my horse? I'll ride Thunder back."

"No, I can handle Thunder just fine. Our issue was the heavy rain. Besides, wasn't his father who caused your accident?"

Rori pulls back as if he's been sucker-punched. "Who told you about my accident?"

I bite my lower lip. I shouldn't have said anything. "Lizzy did. I'm sorry."

My stomach drops through the earth as I take in Rori's distressed expression. His jaw is locked tight, his eyebrows are furrowed together, but it's the sadness in his eyes that makes my chest feel hollow. I want to pull him close and try to erase the memories that are causing him so much pain. But I do none of that, too afraid he'll reject me, push me away.

"Let's get back to the house." He turns away, heading for his horse.

My heart is as heavy as lead now, a complete contrast to what I was feeling not too long ago. I climb onto Thunder, wincing when my naked legs meet the cold bite of wet leather. Rori leads the way, and once we're out of the forest, we break into a trot. Soon the farmhouse looms over the rise and makes me realize I could've made it back on my own if I hadn't been so afraid to get lost.

Both Rori and I dismount just outside the stable. My hospital sling is in shambles now, so I pull it off, bunch it together into a tight ball, and throw it into a nearby garbage can. Then I lead Thunder to his stall, but Rori once again tries to take the horse away from me.

I move the rein out of his reach. "I can do it."

"Why are you being stubborn right now? You're half naked

and your lips are purple again. Get back into the house." He tries to level me with a glare, but I'm holding my ground. I won't be intimidated by him.

I'm being difficult on purpose, a total bitch move on my part, especially when I was the one who hurt him with my slipup. This is a classic Emma Hart defensive mechanism: push him away before he can do that to me. I was supposed to leave my bad habits behind during this trip. Finding Declan was my path to redemption, but it seems old habits are impossible to break.

"Don't tell me what to do," I say a little louder, and Thunder whinnies in complaint. I pat his nose, then lead him to his place.

One thing I could use Rori's help with is unsaddling the horse, but I'm too proud and I won't ask for it. I get on with the task instead, clenching my jaw to prevent my teeth from rattling too loudly. My entire body is shaking, it's so damn cold here, and it's taking me forever with the use of only one hand. Eventually, Rori comes to see what's taking me so long, and without saying a word, he helps with the unbuckling and then removes the heavy saddle. I wouldn't have managed to do that on my own, but at least he didn't make me ask for his help.

The stall is already small, and with Rori's presence, it feels like a broom closet. He goes out first, carrying the saddle with him, and I take the opportunity to flee, marching out of the stable and then sprinting toward the main house. I'm cold, irritated, and remorseful. And now I'm about to add mortified to that list too by walking into Rori's parents' home without any pants on.

When I come into the foyer, the first person who finds me is Rori's aunt. She gives me a quick glance, notices my naked legs, and without a comment about it, steers me toward the stairs.

"Go on now before the entire family finds out you're back."

"Thanks," I say, right before I sprint to the second floor.

Once in my room, my eyes immediately zero in on the bed. The memories imprinted on those sheets are as vivid as ever. So is the second round in that cabin.

With a groan, I head to the bathroom, locking the door behind me and leaning against the hard surface. I'm facing the mirror above the sink, and my reflection is cringe-worthy to say the least. My hair is messy and flat against my skull, the only colors on my pale face the smeared mascara under my eyes and the redness around my lips where the skin was rubbed raw from Rori's kisses. I'm glad it was Rori's aunt who found me in this state, and not his mother. I think the woman actually likes me. I'm still unsure about the others. Lizzy is definitely not my fan.

I pull my sweater off, then get rid of my underwear. The shower knob creaks when I turn it, and at first the water is icy. It takes almost a minute for it to finally warm up. I take my time under the stream, letting the hot jets thaw me out. When the bone-deep cold has finally gone way, I wash my hair twice, then repeat the process with conditioner. By the time I'm done with my extremely long cleaning ritual, the bathroom is shrouded in steam.

Since I forgot to bring a change of clothes with me to the bathroom, I wrap my body in a towel and return to the room. Rori isn't here, thank God. Remembering the comment he made about my jeans, I choose a snug woolen dress instead. It's nice, warm, and hugs my curves in all the right places. I'm not trying to impress the man. Not at all.

I let out loud snort. *I'm so full of it.*

I only dry my hair with a towel because I have no patience to spend another half hour blow-drying it. Ready, I head downstairs, following the sound of voices. His family is congregated in the spacious living room. To my ultimate surprise, Lizzy jumps off the couch, heads my way, and hugs me.

"I'm so sorry I left you back there. I didn't mean to lose you in the rain, I swear."

She must've forgotten about my arm, which is now lying limp by my side and being crushed by her hug. Not knowing what to do, I pat her back and slowly disengage.

My eyes find Rori, standing next to the fireplace with his head down. His hair is damp, which means he must've used the shower in another room. Duh, with the way I hogged our bathroom, he had to find an alternative. He won't meet my gaze, though, which feels worse than any angry words he could throw my way.

"It's okay, Lizzy," I say. "I know you didn't do it on purpose. All is well."

She nods and returns to her seat.

Keira claps her hands together, commanding everyone's attention. "Good. Now that a tragedy has been averted, I can share the news." She looks pointedly at me. "Dad found Rori's old yearbook." The smile on her face is victorious when she hands me a thick book. "I marked the page with Martin D. Kelly's picture already."

Not knowing what to say, I open the book and quickly find the man in question. Yep, it's him all right. I'm one step closer to my goal, but I'm so underwhelmed by it, it's not even funny. I don't want Declan, not when I think I already have what I'm looking for.

I lift my face, hoping Rori will look my way, but he doesn't.

"So, I made some calls," Keira continues. "And I got an address for you."

Her words give me pause. Blinking to focus on her face, I say, "Wait, you called him without knowing he was the right man?"

She shrugs. "I had a hunch he was the right guy. Besides, I was friends with his sister, so it wasn't a big deal. I didn't call him, I called her."

The smile on Keira's face is genuine. She's waiting for my reply, but I can't summon the will to do the right thing, which is to thank her profoundly. Her smile eventually wilts with my lack of response, and then someone says I'm too stunned for words.

Finally, after shaking my head in an attempt to kick-start my brain, I find my voice. "Thank you, Keira. I really appreciate it."

"No problem. If you want to catch him, you'd better go today. It seems he's leaving the country again tomorrow morning."

"Does he know I'm coming?" I ask, unable to disguise the panic in my voice. This situation is getting completely out of control.

Keira shakes her head. "No. Lara, Declan's sister, knew exactly who you were. It seems her brother was trying to locate you as well. We both agreed that it would better if you surprised him. If you weren't Rori's girlfriend, I'd say that would be the perfect setup for a rom-com."

Rori makes a disgruntled noise in the back of his throat, drawing Keira's attention to him.

"Gee, will you relax? I'm not saying Emma should ditch you for the guy."

I'm screaming in my head. Without knowing, Keira guessed exactly what I was planning to do not too long ago. This morning, my resolution wasn't so set in stone anymore, and now I don't know what I want. There's an ache in my heart, no doubt put there by my unresolved status with Rori. Is that a sign that anything between us will only result in more pain?

While I'm having an internal freak-out, Rori finally looks in my direction. "I'm ready if you are. He's in Galway. It's a few hours away from here."

His cold, emotionless tone puts another hole in my heart. So with an equally detached voice, I say, "Let's go, then."

22

———

EMMA

We've been on the road for half an hour and Rori hasn't spoken a word to me. I'd like to say it's for the best, but the silence is killing me. I look out the window, trying to appreciate the view, but I keep replaying everything that happened this morning: the take-no-prisoners sex in the cabin, the discovery that Rori had seen me at my worst, his reaction at me mentioning his past.

"That's it. I can't take it anymore," I turn to him.

"What?" he grumbles, his facial expression neutral.

"This toxic air surrounding us. I hate it, so I think we should clear it."

"Toxic air? I didn't notice."

Turning my eyes into slits, I have the urge to smack him upside the head. "Stop being obtuse. Something is obviously eating at you."

His nostrils flare as he clenches his jaw hard. He keeps his eyes on the road when he replies, "There's nothing eating at me. Abso-fucking-lutely nothing."

"The fact that you inserted 'fucking' in your answer says otherwise. Listen, I am truly, truly sorry that I mentioned your accident. I should've stopped Lizzy when she started talking about your past, but I—" I look out the window again when the sudden lump in my throat threatens to choke me. *What's wrong with me?*

"But what?" Rori asks, softer now.

"I couldn't help wanting to know more. It made me feel closer to you somehow." I shake my head. "Shit, listen to what I'm saying. I sound so cliché. Anyway, I know what it's like to have a part of yourself that you want to keep hidden from everyone."

"You think I'm mad at you because of that? If anything, I'm angry at Lizzy for having such a big mouth."

"So why haven't you been able to look me in the eyes since the cabin?"

I watch his profile, noticing how his muscles are tense around his mouth. "I didn't know how much she'd told you, Emma. And you're right, there's a side of me that I don't want you to ever see."

The naked truth in that statement, the raw pain I hear embedded in those words, brings tears to my eyes. I've gone from never crying to a blubbering mess in the span of days. *What is Rori doing to me?*

"More than understandable." I force the words out. "That was a life-altering moment. I don't know anyone who would go through that with a smile on their face."

Rori's face is still a cold mask, and his knuckles are white from holding the steering wheel too tight. I want to touch him, to let him know he can talk to me, but something in his demeanor keeps me from reaching out.

"If we had planned this better, we could go sight-seeing," I say in attempt to lighten the mood.

Rori snorts. "Are you telling me you're not in a hurry to see your precious Declan?"

The sarcasm in Rori's answer is what finally makes everything click in my head. He's not upset because his sister blabbed, at least not anymore. He's upset because he's driving me to see another man, the guy I foolishly believed could be the only one to wake up my dead heart. *I'm such an idiot!*

"Rori, pull over."

"What?" He looks at me, alarmed. "Are you sick?"

"No. Just pull over."

"What for?"

"Stop asking questions and do it," I snap.

With a groan, he turns on the hazard blinkers and pulls to the side of the road. We're in the middle of nowhere, no sign of civilization for miles on end.

"What's going on?" Rori turns to me. "And why are you looking at me like I did something terrible?"

Irritated and also not knowing exactly what to do now, I get out of the car in a huff, stomping on the wild grass that lines the side of the road.

"Emma!" Rori yells and I turn, folding my good arm over the improvised sling I fashioned out of a scarf. "Bloody hell. Could you please fucking quit with the drama already?" he asks when he stops in front of me.

"I'm not being dramatic. I'm just frustrated."

"Great. That makes two of us."

"What do you want from me, Rori?"

My question seems to catch him off-guard, and the anger in his gaze dims. He runs his hand over his hair and looks out in the distance. "It doesn't matter what I want."

I move closer and pinch his chin between my thumb and forefinger, turning his face back to mine. "I think it's high time we stop playing childish games and are honest with one another."

"You want honesty? I'd rather be anywhere else than driving you to Galway to be reunited with your maybe soul mate. I'm dying of jealousy. There, honest enough for you?"

"Yes," I reply softly while my heart pounds inside my chest.

"Don't worry, Emma. I'll still drive you there because a deal is a deal."

"What if I told you I don't want you to drive me there."

"What?"

"You heard me. Everything happened so fast. First I remembered about the night I made a complete fool of myself in front of you, and then you got upset that I knew about your accident. I just didn't have the chance to tell you that...." I pause and look at the ground, unable to finish the sentence. *Why is it so hard for me to say that I want to be with him?*

"Tell me what, Em?" Rori's voice is much softer now. With a finger under my chin, he forces me to look into his eyes. "What do you want to tell me?"

"I'm not sure what's going on between us, Rori. I can't describe a feeling I've never felt before, but...." I place my hand over his chest, feeling his accelerated heartbeat. "I want more from you than just sex."

His lips curl into a sexy-as-hell grin. "Are you saying you want to be my girlfriend for real?"

"Please don't use that word. It's so... confining."

He palms my cheek and his grin turns into a full-bloom smile. "I'll make you love it."

My brain immediately latches onto the word 'love,' sending my body into panic mode. My heart isn't just accelerated, it's thundering inside my chest, and the urge to flee is damn real.

The fear vanishes like it was never there when Rori lowers his lips to mine and kisses me like he's doing it for the first time. It's tender, sweet, and full of promises. I wrap my arm around his trim waist, needing to bring us even closer together. I can't help noticing how well my body fits with his frame, like he was made for me.

Rori captures my face between his hands, as if he's afraid I'm going to slip away. Then his arms wrap around my back, going lower and lower until both of his hands are resting on the base of my spine. A tendril of pleasure curls there before expanding through the rest of my body.

A loud horn has my heart jumping up my throat and I pull back. Rori curses under his breath as he stares at the car speeding away out in the distance. It seems someone thought it was funny to interrupt our moment.

"Jerks," I say.

A light breeze pushes strands of my hair over my face, and I try keeping it out of my eyes and mouth to no avail. With a chuckle, Rori pulls the whole thing back and ties it in a ponytail. Hmm, it's kind of nice having a guy with long hair around.

"There. Much better." He smiles.

"Thank you."

We lock gazes and I'm caught in a whirlwind of emotions as I stare into his eyes. I don't know what's happening to me. I've felt the rush of a new fling before, the euphoria, but it usually went away after sex. I've never experienced the emotion lasting longer, lingering. No, lingering isn't the correct word, more like expanding.

Hold up. Don't jump the gun just yet, Emma. Falling in love doesn't necessarily mean loving someone. And that's what I promised my father, that I'd find a person to grow with, not someone to warm my bed for a few months.

But as I continue to stare into Rori's eyes, I feel my heart swell and overflow with something extraordinary, a giddy sensation stronger than a mere crush. I can't help but wonder if he'll be an extended booty call, or if he'll be my forever.

"What now?" he asks.

"Hmm?"

"Should we continue on our way to Galway, or should we head back?"

The purpose of our trip. Declan. It all comes back to me like a pesky dark cloud wanting to rain on my parade. It's all my damn fault, so I can't complain.

I let out a heavy sigh. "Well, we can't just turn back after your sister went through all the trouble. I think seeing him again might be good for me. It might help make sense of what happened that day, you know?"

"Yeah, I hear ya."

"But if you don't want to meet him, it's okay."

He kisses me softly on the lips before he replies, "I was only jealous when I thought he was my competition. I'd like to thank the guy for saving your life that day."

"Really? Do you think you'd be okay if maybe we spent the night in Galway?"

"Why wouldn't I be okay with that?"

"Well, for starters, we didn't bring anything with us besides the clothes on our backs. And I don't know if your family will be upset since they haven't seen you in a long time."

"Trust me, Em, my family is not an issue. Besides, the last thing I'm worried about is clothes. In fact, I don't think we'll be spending much time wearing them."

My lips curl into smile. I'm loving this unrestrained, naughty side of Rori. "Oh yeah? How come?"

Rori kisses me again, then brings his lips to my ear. "I have plans for you, Emma Hart, and that includes tasting every single curve and edge of your body. Clothing is most definitely a no-go."

23

RORI

Three hours and fifty minutes. That's how it long it takes to go from Kinsale to Galway if you take the most direct path and ignore all the places you could stop for sight-seeing. Despite Emma's suggestion earlier that maybe we could do that, neither of us mentioned it again once we got back on the road. Truth be told, I can't wait to get this meeting with Declan out of the way. We can take a more scenic route on the way back.

Emma's hand is casually resting on my thigh while she's distracted with the view. But my cock doesn't care about that, and it's standing at attention. I'm tempted to stop the car so I can kiss her some more, but I don't think only kissing will suffice. No, I really need Emma naked under me, on top of me, anyway she'd like. Basically I just want her naked. Period.

It's easier to get lost in the physical aspect of what's happening between us than in the fact that my heart is just as excited as my dick is—maybe even more. It hasn't stopped pounding since Emma told me she wants to give us a try. I should be cautious. I'm not foolish enough to believe Emma isn't at flight risk. She doesn't believe she can fall in love with anyone, which leaves me in a precarious situation since I know I'm falling head over heels for her. I knew she'd be dangerous and yet I couldn't stop going deeper, couldn't stop wanting more.

We arrive in Galway by midafternoon, and the loud rumbling in my belly reminds me that we haven't eaten anything since we left. Emma must be hungry too, but she hasn't said anything about it. The easy smile she had on her face has now vanished, and I catch a hint of tension there. This encounter can't be easy for her, and maybe she didn't realize the implications until now.

"Hey, do you want to grab a bite to eat real quick before we text Declan's sister to say we're on our way?"

Emma shakes her head. "No. I don't think I can eat anything right now. Please don't take this the wrong way, but I'm a bundle of nerves."

I squeeze her hand, then lace our fingers together. "Don't worry. I understand this isn't easy for you."

"No, it really isn't. God, there are so many details about that day I don't remember. I'm not sure if Declan will want to talk about it, or…." She looks away. "I have half a mind to call the whole thing off. I'm such a coward."

"Hey, don't say that. You're not a coward. You went through a terrible experience that no one should have to endure. What you're feeling is normal. You're not a coward. You're one of the bravest people I know."

"What? You can't possibly say that."

"I can and I am saying that. You went through hell and you're still able to laugh, to appreciate your friends and family. That takes courage, Em. Trust me, I know."

"How come I have the feeling we're no longer only talking about me."

Shit, I've said too much. "Never mind that. What I'm trying to say is if you don't feel up to seeing Declan, we don't have to. I won't think you're a coward for changing your mind, and you shouldn't either."

She watches me as if she wants to read my mind, but she doesn't pry. It doesn't change the fact that I'm not being fair here. Emma has bared her soul to me more than once, while the only piece of information she has about me is what she got from my sister. She needs to know what she's getting herself into. But one thing at the time.

"Okay, let's text Declan's sister, then."

Emma asks for her phone number and shoots off a quick message. Her phone rings a minute later. "She's calling me back," she tells me before answering the call, putting it on speaker. "Hello?"

"Hi, Emma. This is Lara, Declan's sister. I'm so sorry to tell you this, but there's been a change of plans and my brother had to leave town earlier than he thought. I just learned this a few minutes ago."

"Oh," Emma says. She sounds disappointed, but her expression seems relieved. "That's too bad."

"I feel terrible. I should've just told him you're coming. Gah, I want to kick myself. How long are you staying in Ireland?"

"For another nine days."

"I have no idea what Declan's plans are, but if it's all right with you, I'll let him know you're in town. Maybe he can come back home sooner."

"I don't want him to change his plans on my account."

"Don't be silly. He'd love to see you. You made quite an impression on my brother. I'm kind of a bit upset that you're with Rori." Lara chuckles, but I don't find her comment the least bit amusing.

Emma looks at me apologetically. "Actually, Rori's with me right now, staring daggers at the phone."

"Oh my goodness. Am I on speaker phone? Rori, I was just kidding."

I roll my eyes. "Yeah, yeah, you're real funny. No wonder you and my sister are friends."

"Hmm, I don't what to make of that statement. Anyway, I'd invite you over for drinks, but I got a sick kid on my hands. Are you planning to stay in Galway for the night at least?"

I stare at Emma, who's watching me curiously. "Yes, that's the plan."

"Let me know if you need suggestions for where to go to dinner or help finding lodging. I can make some calls."

"Thanks, Lara. I hope to meet in person someday so I can give you a proper stare-down."

"Duly noted. Take care, and Emma, I'm so sorry."

Emma says her goodbyes and ends the call.

"So, if Lara and Keira were friends, and Declan went to the same school as your sister, how come you said you didn't know him when I asked?"

"Because I didn't. Keira is two years older than me, and we didn't hang in the same crowd. I was training or with... well, I was busy."

"You were going to say with Alannah, weren't you?"

"Yes. Emma, you don't have to worry about her, okay? I'm over her, have been over for almost ten years. She's so in the past you'd need an archeological crew to dig her out."

"Okay, I believe you. Now back to the question at hand. What should we do?"

"I'd say finding a hotel is the first order of business. With St. Paddy's Day just around the corner, I'm afraid a lot of places will be booked."

"Would you mind terribly if I got us a room in a five-star hotel? It might increase our chances, and their king-size beds are wicked." She bounces her eyebrows and up and down, making me laugh.

"When you put it like, how can I say no?"

24

─────────

EMMA

Okay, I'm back to feeling like a coward. The moment Lara said Declan wasn't around, a wave of relief ran through me. I can't believe that in all the weeks I spent prepping for this trip, I never considered the actual ramifications of seeing the man who saved my life face-to-face. What would it do to my psyche? Would Declan trigger an even stronger panic attack? I'm sure my therapist would be the one cheering this idea the most, but I'm so fucking glad it didn't happen and it wasn't by my doing.

Since Rori let me pick the hotel, I called the one at the top of my list, a boutique hotel at the heart of Galway that gets great reviews. Without a budget limit, I splurge, using the black Amex Dad gave me when I turned eighteen. My closest friends used to ask if I ever felt guilty about spending my father's money, and the reason why I don't is because if I didn't spend, it would break his heart. It sounds like the perfect excuse, but I know my father and how he feels about not having enough time to spend with me. Letting me splurge on his dime is his way to compensate for all the time lost. I don't think he'll ever stop pampering me even when I have a real job, making real money.

As we enter the lavish hotel room, Rori whistles, looking at the modern, sleek décor mixed with lavish, classic feature pieces, such as the deep burgundy wall behind the hotel's reception desk. The white and shiny check-in counter is a stark contrast to the bold color. A friendly clerk smiles with perfect white teeth when I approach and says all the right things that I'm sure he's tired of repeating.

I give him my name, and with speedy efficiency we're checked in less than five minutes later. Most tourists would just drop off their things and go explore the city, but not me. There's another Irish landscape I'd rather get to know inch by inch.

Inside the elevator, Rori and I stand side by side with only our fingers touching. We're not alone, so the innocent contact is the only thing we allow ourselves. But once inside the privacy of our room, I don't know who jumps whom first. Rori pushes me against the wall, kissing me like he's a starving man. It reminds of the dream I had at the start of our trip, but this time there's no waking up before the best part.

Clothes are pulled and yanked without regard to where they fall. The only time Rori stops and is careful with me is when he removes the scarf around my arm. He then drops to his knees and peppers my stomach with kisses hotter than tamales. My panties are already gone—I don't even remember peeling them off. When Rori kisses the junction where thigh and pelvis meet, I have to hold on to the wall to keep from falling. He lifts my leg over his shoulder, opening me for the sweet invasion, and then it's slick on slick as he suckles and licks my pussy.

I come once, then twice, before Rori lifts me and throws me onto the bed. I'm still riding the wave of multiple orgasms when I feel his head at my entrance, rubber suit on and all. With a powerful thrust, he's inside me at the same time he covers my mouth with his. I grab his shoulders, digging my nails into his flesh as the pleasure down below intensifies with each pounding of his hips against mine. Rori abandons my lips to kiss my neck, and goose bumps flow down my arms.

"I don't want you to ever stop fucking me," I say, glad we're not at his folks' and I can be as a loud as I want.

"I'm sorry, lass," he replies, out of breath. "Eventually I'll have to stop."

He lets out a guttural noise right before his entire frame starts to shake. He pumps into me faster, as if he wants to milk every single drop of his release, and sends me spiraling down again. I scream his name as another powerful orgasm washes over me, leveling me to the ground.

Rori collapses next to me, pulling me against his body as he does. We don't speak for several minutes as we catch our breaths.

"Wow, that was... wow," he says.

"I love your way with words." I laugh.

"Forgive me if I can't be more eloquent. You robbed me of words."

"That's better." I kiss his chest. "I'm never leaving this bed."

"I like that plan." He squeezes me tighter. "But I'd like to take you out. Galway is fun."

I roll in his arms so I can face him. "Are you asking me out on a date?"

He smiles as he studies my face. "Yes, lass. I'm asking you out."

I kiss Rori again because the man is that irresistible. Honestly, I should be rewarded for resisting him so long.

"Is that a yes?" Rori asks against my lips.

"Yes."

"Good." He rolls on top of me and I feel his cock ready for action again. It'll be a miracle if we ever make out of this room before tomorrow.

Rori

Talk about libido on overdrive. It seems I can't get near Emma without wanting to bend her over and take her like I'm a caveman. But it's not only undeniable sexual attraction that has me craving the woman like I've never craved anyone in my life—it's her, period. The way she moves, talks, and laughs. Every time I look at her, a warmth spreads across my chest. She makes everything seem brighter, better.

I love her. That's it, plain and simple. Even when my prejudice tried to get in the way, my heart knew she was the one for me, which has me even more nervous about tonight. Not the first date part, but what comes next. I have to come clean to her about my past. If she's willing to give this relationship a try, she needs to do so with eyes wide open.

I'd prefer to take Emma out to a quiet dinner, but she wanted to experience Galway like a tourist, so we head to The Kings Head, one of the most popular pubs in the city. Located in the heart of Galway's Latin Quarter, the landmark pub has earned a great reputation for live music and comedy, hearty food, and great entertainment over three floors.

For a Monday night, the place is fairly busy, but if we'd come here on the weekend, forget getting through the front door. We manage to snag a high table, and as Emma gets distracted examining the menu, I get distracted staring at her. She's so beautiful it almost hurts. High cheekbones, a small and delicate nose, and my favorite part, those plump and delectable lips that at the moment are curled into a small smile.

"I know you're staring," she says.

"I can't help it."

She brings her gaze to mine. "You know, I thought the same when I first saw you."

I clamp my mouth shut. I don't like to remember that evening. I was so awful to her.

Emma notices my reaction, and covering my hand with hers, she asks, "What's wrong?"

"I hate how I treated you that night."

"Why? As far I can remember, you were amazing. You took me home when you didn't have to. If anyone should feel bad about that evening, it's me. I'm so ashamed." She drops her gaze, but I'm having none of that.

"Hey, you're allowed to have a crazy night with your friends. I'm not judging, I swear."

"But you did." She looks at me, knowing.

"Yes I did, but only because I was so fucking stupid. I was happy to put you in a box so I could ignore how you made me feel the first time I saw you."

"And how was that?"

"Like I'd been sucker-punched."

"That's not a very nice visual." She laughs.

I shake my head. "Ah, I'm terrible with words. Let's just go with when I first saw you, it was like all the air went out."

She narrows her eyes. "That's from a song."

"Guilty."

The levity leaves her eyes and is replaced by seriousness. "I don't do drugs anymore. That night was the last time I touched molly."

Her confession, though unexpected, eases a worry in my heart. I didn't want to ask about her partying habits, afraid to come across like a judgmental ass once again.

I lean forward, stopping an inch away from her lips. "Lass, I'm glad to hear that."

"Holy shit, I'll be damned. If it isn't Rori O'Shea." A voice I haven't heard in almost a decade has my blood running cold.

I turn around as my spine goes taut. Looking at me with a smug smile on his ugly, porky face is Simon Ackerman, the guy who was a thorn in my side my last year in high school, flanked by two guys I don't recognize. They all look shit-faced, though.

Simon was a forward from a rival football team, and he went out of his way to prove he was better than me. But he never succeeded because, for what he had in nastiness, he lacked in talent. Maybe that's why he hated me so much.

"Simon," I say.

"I didn't know you were in the country. The last I heard you were sweeping floors and cleaning toilets in a third-grade pub in America." He laughs with his mates.

"You must be living under a rock all these years, then. Now piss off, Simon."

"Oh, someone still doesn't have a sense of humor." He claps my shoulder, hard, and it takes a Herculean effort on my part not to shove him off me.

"You'd have to be funny for people to find humor in what you say," Emma chimes in, staring daggers at Simon. Ah shit, I was hoping he wouldn't notice her. But of course, that's impossible. Even if she hadn't opened her mouth, how could anyone miss her?

"Oh, Rori has a new girl." Simon leers at her, dropping his beady eyes to her chest. "Hmm, definitely an upgrade from your last one."

I stand up and tower over the guy. He reeks of beer and rotten meat. "You'd better leave now, Simon."

"What's the matter, Rori? Are you afraid I'm going to take that one away like I did Alannah?"

"What the fuck are you talking about?"

"Oh, you didn't know? Alannah and I were fucking like bunnies while you were recovering from your accident."

I know I shouldn't listen to Simon—he's scum and a fucking liar—but the idea of Alannah betraying me like that, and with a guy I despise, makes my stomach churn. I go back in time and remember how different Alannah became after my entire future went down the drain. She turned distant, fidgety even. It wouldn't a surprise if she were cheating.

"Classy, Simon. Very classy."

From the corner of my eye, I see a beefy guy wearing a muscle shirt coming our way. I return to my seat because getting kicked out on account of a fucktard like Simon isn't worth it.

"Is there a problem here?" the bouncer asks, eyeing Simon with clear disgust.

"No problem at all, sir. I was just saying hello to an old friend."

"Okay. Either take a seat or move along. You're blocking the way."

Simon twists his face into a scowl before heading off to the bar. Not far enough, in my opinion.

I look at Emma and find her watching me with an odd glint in her eyes. I have no idea what to make of it, but one thing is certain: Simon has definitely pissed all over my romantic evening with her, and for that reason alone, I want to punch him in the throat.

"I'm sorry about that."

"Me too. That guy was...." She shivers. "He reminded me of the asshole who assaulted me in your pub."

Guilt and regret mix in my chest. "I'm so sorry that happened, Em."

"Crap, I shouldn't have said anything. I don't want you to feel responsible for it. Shit happens all the time."

I open my mouth to protest, but she covers my lips with her forefinger. "Shh. Enough bad juju. Let's order something. I'm famished." She gives me a smile but it doesn't reach her eyes, and I curse Simon again.

25

EMMA

THE GUY WAS AN ASSHOLE, NO DOUBT, BUT HE WOULDN'T HAVE completely ruined my evening if I hadn't witnessed the change in Rori's demeanor when his ex-girlfriend was mentioned. The blood rushed from his face as he looked at Simon with murder in his gaze. I know I was being irrational—I would've been taken aback as well if I learned a boyfriend had cheated on me —but there's not rationalization when hearts and feelings are involved.

So I forced myself to pretend everything was okay, but from time to time, I caught Rori throwing a hard glance at the asshole from his past, a guy who used to play on an opposing team, I learned. It was like Rori couldn't help himself; not even when the band started to play and I dragged him to the dance floor did he relax his stance.

Ready to call the evening, I head to the bathroom before we catch an Uber back to the hotel. I take my time reapplying my lipstick and fixing my hair because I want to perfect my expression of everything being fine.

The moment I step back into the pub, I know something's amiss. There's a commotion out front where a cluster of people has formed. I hastily search for Rori, finding our table vacant. I can't find Simon and his cronies either, and a bad feeling settles in the pit of my stomach.

I stride toward the front of the pub and elbow my way through the throng of people until I manage to get outside. Then I freeze in my tracks. Rori's being held in a headlock by the bouncer who approached our table earlier. His hair is loose and wild, and there's blood running from the corner of his mouth.

Simon is lying on the street, holding the side of his face. His friends try to help him get up, but he shoves them off.

Rori turns to me and stops struggling. The bouncer whispers something in his ear, and Rori nods. Then the bouncer lets him go.

"Emma—"

I raise my hand. "Save it, Rori. Let's get back to the hotel. I'm tired."

"I'm sorry."

I ignore him because if I say anything, I might start crying. No matter which angle I see this situation from, Rori got into a fight over his ex, which means he's clearly not over her as he claims to be. I'm not even surprised. First loves are the relationships that never go away, that leave a permanent mark. I should know because Rori being my first love will be forever imprinted in my heart.

The bitter realization just makes everything more devastating. I love him. Truly, deeply, madly, and I hate, absolutely fucking *hate* that I'll never be the love that brands his soul. Alannah is that woman. Even if he no longer loves her, she'll always be his first love.

Don't be ridiculous, Emma. Everyone has a past.

My dependable brain comes to the rescue, stomping on the stupid. Too bad it can't do anything about the ache in my chest.

Rori doesn't try to make conversation during the ride home.

Instead, he keeps staring out the window. He cleaned the blood from his face, at least. Once out of the car, we proceed the funeral procession through the deserted hotel lobby. I'm no longer on the verge of crying, which is good because crying in front of Rori would be the worst thing I could do. Yeah, yeah, I'm fucking quoting Rizzo here, but there's no surprise since she and I could be the same person.

Rori hangs back once we're out of the elevator and remains at a good distance during the silent walk down the hall. I unlock our door without consciously doing so. Our suite no longer has the warmth it had before. It's cold, sterile, monotone. Or maybe that's just a reflection of what I'm feeling.

I don't know what to do, how to behave, and Rori seems just as lost as I am. Maybe he realized the same thing I did—he hasn't moved on, and hooking up with me was a colossal mistake. He sits on the edge of the bed while I remain standing, leaning against the sleek dresser opposite the bed.

He leans his elbows on his knees and clutches his head before looking at me.

"You deserve an explanation," he says.

"I think I know what you're going to say. And it's cool. I understand." I shrug, faking nonchalance. But I'm screaming in my head, *How dare you dangle your love in front of my face only to take it away the next second?*

"Whatever it is you think you know, it's wrong."

"Rori, I get it. You got upset to learn Alannah cheated on you with that jerk. I would be upset and jealous too if I were in your shoes."

Rori shakes his head and stares at the floor. "You're wrong, so very wrong."

I open my mouth to rebuff his statement, but Rori stares at me again and speaks before I can. "I was upset, of course. Simon was a sneaky bastard back when we were teens, and he turned into an even bigger jerk as an adult. But whether he slept with Alannah or not wasn't the reason I smashed his face in. He was disrespecting my family, and when he made a lewd comment about you, I just snapped."

I stand a little straighter and uncross my legs. "You got into a fight because of me?"

"Well, when you say it like that, it makes me sound a little extreme, but...." He rubs his face and his eyes glaze over. "It wouldn't be a lie."

His shoulders sag forward as he lets out a loud exhale. "I tried to kill myself."

I stop breathing for a second, and my heart seems to stop too, only to lurch into my throat. "When?" I ask, but I already know the answer.

"After the accident, I went into a very dark place. Football had been my entire world since I was a wee lad. My father played in his glory days, and the sport became our bonding time. He was so proud of me when my team would win a game, and he'd reward me with extra treats based on the number of goals I scored. When he realized I wasn't only good but had a real shot of making it to the big leagues, things became more intense. All he cared about was making sure I was training enough, eating right. It was almost like I stopped being his son and became his project."

"That must not have been easy," I say.

"No. At the time, I didn't think much about it. He was my hero, and I wanted to make him proud. I didn't see that his interest in my career had become an obsession. When the accident happened, the first thing my father asked the doctor was how soon I could play again. He didn't ask if I was in pain or want to know exactly what happened. He just wanted to know when I could go back on the field."

Rori's voice breaks at the end, and so does my heart. With tear-filled eyes, I go to him, sitting by his side and leaning my head against his shoulder. He laces our fingers together, keeping our joined hands over his lap.

"When the doctor told him my recovery would be lengthy and it was likely I'd never play like I used to, the disappointment I saw in his gaze crushed me. Depression took over, and one day I decided to end it all."

"How?"

"I got hold of sleeping pills through a shady character I knew from school. I waited until I was alone in the house and swallowed several with the help of whiskey. If Keira hadn't forgotten her ID, I wouldn't be here." Rori turns to me, his eyes red and brimmed with tears. A lonely one escapes, rolling down his cheek. I kiss it away, then continue peppering his face with kisses while holding his face between my hands.

I feel moisture on my cheek and realize I'm crying too. Leaning my forehead against his, I say, "I'm so glad you failed, Rori. So fucking glad, you have no idea. Thanks for telling me."

"I couldn't be with you without revealing my darkest sin, Emma. It wouldn't be fair."

I ease back and stare into his eyes, finding in them passion, humility, love. Now would be the right time to tell him how I feel, to say I love you. But the words lodge in my throat, the deep-seated fear grasping my heart in a vicious hold again. I settle for the next best thing.

"Make love to me, Rori."

His eyes drop to my lips, then to the base of my throat. His arms move around my neck to undo the knot holding my scarf. He moves my arm out of the way, gently as to not cause me any pain, before untying the sash holding my wrap dress together. The silky fabric parts, revealing nothing but naked skin. Rori sucks in a breath before leaning down and sucking one of my nipples into his mouth. I throw my head back, running my hand through his hair, pulling at the strands. Heat pools between my legs, and with a soft touch, he slides his fingers down my belly until they disappear inside my underwear. When his finger sweeps against my clit, I jump a little.

"I love how wet you get for me, lass."

He strokes me again and I almost lose my grip on reality. His touch feels so damn good. Panting, I curl my hands over the fabric of his sleeve, twisting it as much as I can.

"More fingers, Rori. Please?"

"You asked me to make love to you, Em, and that means I'm going to take things very, very slowly."

He pushes my body onto the bed and then continues his sweet torture. My panties are peeled off my legs excruciatingly slowly, and by the time he returns to my aching bundle of nerves, I'm on the verge of finishing the job myself. But all good things come for those who wait, and Rori's tongue is one of those wicked good things. He parts my folds with his fingers and then sucks my clit into his mouth. Fuck taking things slowly—I come hard on his tongue, and he takes everything with gusto, if his moan is any indication.

My eyes are still closed when he begins the journey back up my body, kissing and licking as he goes. As much as I love the way Rori seems to already know every sensitive spot on my body, I also want to give him as much pleasure as he's giving me. All those years of practice have to be good for something.

I lock my legs behind his ass and roll us around in a swift move, finding no resistance on his part. Straddling him now, I rub my sex against his erection, and Rori's eyes close halfway. He grabs my hips, rotating his own to increase the friction.

"You like to keep control, don't you, Rori?"

He chuckles, and it's the most glorious sound after the confession that must've cost him so much to make. "Sometimes."

"Me too." I gyrate my hips and the head of his cock goes in.

"I'm not wearing protection."

I close my eyes and impale myself a little more in him. "I know, but you feel so good."

"I'm clean."

Opening my eyes again, I watch him watch me. His hair is fanned over the plush pillow, giving him an even wilder look. "Me too, and I'm on the pill."

I've never slept with anyone without protection. It was a rule I vowed to follow, not only because I sure as hell didn't want to end up knocked up by a random guy, but because hello, STDs. The fact that I'm more than willing to break my rule with Rori speaks volumes. I not only love him, I'm willing to commit to him, which in my world don't necessarily come together.

"Are you sure?" he asks.

In answer, I bring my pelvis all the way down, pushing his entire length into me. And oh my God, he feels amazing. I never knew what a difference it'd make without the condom. I ride him slowly, trying to savor the sensation, but Rori's getting too impatient. He sits up, tangles his fingers in my hair, and brings my lips to his.

The penetration changes at this new angle, making going slowly not an option but a must. He doesn't seem to mind because he's taking control of my mouth now, devouring it, taking possession as he pleases. We keep at it, giving and taking in equal measures. If that's not the definition of compromising, I don't know what is. I don't know who comes first, I only know that we're both riding the wave together and I feel whole for the first time.

I've found my person.

26

RORI

I can't stop smiling like a fool as I drive back to Kinsale. We decided to take the Wild Atlantic Route, which delayed us a couple of hours, but we couldn't go to Galway and not stop at Cliffs of Moher, one of the most beautiful places on Earth. It wasn't Emma's first time there, but it was her first time with me, and I'd like to believe that it held a special meaning to her. I may be putting the cart before the horse, but I can't hold the excitement back.

My only regret is that we couldn't stay longer. I could spend the entire day on those cliffs, looking out at the ocean, feeling the breeze on my face. Sunset is also the best time to be there, as it's one of the most spectacular views you get to see anywhere in Ireland. But I know if we don't get back to Kinsale today, Mum will have a conniption. So I promised Emma we'd return one day. She didn't balk at the idea, which I took as a good sign.

As I turn onto the road that leads to the B&B, I feel a little morose that my time alone with Emma is coming to an end. It's a shitty thing to feel since I haven't seen my family in years, but I can't help it. Or maybe it's the fear that Emma will change her mind and bolt. Knowing what I do about her, how she's viewed relationships for the longest time, I'd be fucking naïve to believe she's completely changed.

When I pull in front of the main building, I'm not surprised that there aren't many cars around. The wedding's in less than a week, and I'm sure the entire family has been conscripted into helping with last-minute details. I don't even want to imagine what impossible task Keira is going to throw my way. Thank fuck Clemmot isn't a social pariah and I don't have to stand in as his best man. I just have to attend his bachelor party and make sure things don't get out of hand, meaning Clemmot doesn't do anything that will warrant the removal of his balls by my dear sister.

I pull Emma to me as we walk toward to the front door, wanting to prolong our closeness. Before we walk in, I spin her around, holding her by the waist. We're kissing before we know it, the heat instantaneous and intense, as if we hadn't made love a few times this morning—in bed, in the shower, against the wall. I know this insatiable hunger will fade eventually, but I don't think I'll ever stop wanting this woman. She's gotten under my skin, branded herself on my soul.

We ease back for air, my heart beating out of sync just like I bet hers is too. "God, I wish we didn't have to go in," I say.

"Family obligations first, fecking later." She tries to imitate my accent, failing adorably.

"*Fecking*?" I laugh.

"No good?" She raises an eyebrow.

"The action? Fecking good. The accent? Not so much."

She hits my chest with the back of her hand, and a bubble of laughter escapes her lips. The sound is infectious, and we're still laughing as we enter the house together. But it doesn't take long for us to notice something is wrong. Harsh voices can be heard coming from the living room. Someone's also crying— Lizzy I think.

I lock gazes with Emma before we head toward the noise. I find my father pacing in front of the fireplace while my mother sits on chair with a dejected, dead expression in her eyes. Lizzy's crying her eyes out on Keira's shoulder.

"You should've told us, Dad." Keira stares hard at our father.

"I thought I had more time. I didn't want to worry your mother needlessly."

"What's going on?" I ask, since no one seems to notice Emma and I are in the room.

"Rori. You're back!" Lizzy jumps off the couch and runs into my arms.

"The bank called and said they were moving up the date the payment is due. I have until next week to come up with the money."

"What? They can't do that," I say.

"Yes they can when their director is that odious Donald Ackerman." Keira spits out the name with so much venom, it would probably burn a hole through the floor.

"Simon's father? He's the bank's director?" I rub my face as things begin to make sense. This can't be a coincidence. "That son of a bitch."

"Rori!" Mum snaps out of her paralysis. "Language, please."

"What does Simon have anything to do with Dad having to pay the bank fifty thousand euros by next Monday?" Keira narrows her eyes at me.

"I bumped into him in Galway last night, and we got into a fight."

"Wait, are you saying Simon got this father to change the terms of a contract in an act of revenge? That can't be legal," Emma chimes in.

Ah fuck. I so didn't want her embroiled in my family's problems.

My father shakes his head, shoving his hands in his pockets and glancing down. I've never seen him act like that, not even when he learned I'd never be the football star he wanted me to be. His sagging shoulders show a man who's accepted defeat.

"Well, Monday was the original date on the contract. I asked for an extension, which the bank agreed on," he says.

"But that's in writing, right?" I ask. "You signed a new contract with the new terms."

When Dad doesn't answer, I curse under my breath.

"Emma's rich. What if she lends us the money?" Lizzy turns to Emma, looking hopeful. "You would lend us the money, right?"

Emma doesn't answer right away; instead, she looks at me and seems conflicted. Our earlier arguments were all the result of her splurging on me with money she didn't earn. As my feelings for her evolved, I pushed that little detail about her to the side, but now I'm afraid what her answer will be. I know fifty thousand euros is nothing to her. Hell, it's probably her minimum monthly expenditure on that black Amex of hers. But taking her money wouldn't feel right.

"I'm sorry, Lizzy. I'm not rich, my father is," Emma replies, and even though her answer won't help this fucked situation, I'm relieved by it.

Of course, no one shares my sentiment, especially Lizzy, who stares at Emma with bright eyes and squashed hope. "But you could ask him for it, right?"

"Lizzy, stop this nonsense. What is Emma going to think about our family? That we're swindlers, or worse, beggars?" Mum says.

"So what does that mean? You're going to lose the B&B?" Keira asks, tearful.

"No. Absolutely not." Emma takes a step forward with chin held high and eyes full of determination.

I've witnessed this side of her before when she was defending her idea to look for Declan. That feels like a thousand years ago.

"First things first," she continues. "I'd like to read the contract. My father is a damn good lawyer, and he taught me how to properly read any legal document, to look for words that can be misleading or have double meaning."

"I had my lawyer go over the contract already. He found nothing that can help," my father replies, already on the defensive.

"Oh, Gerard, I love you, but John Murphy should've retired a decade ago. His mind isn't as sharp as it once was," Mum tells him.

"What does Rori's girlfriend know about Irish law, though." Dad crosses his arms, jutting his chin stubbornly. "No offense, lass."

"For fuck's sake, Dad, let Emma read the contract. I'd like to go over it as well. You asked for my help, didn't you?"

Keira turns to me with mouth agape. "You knew?"

"I told Rori two days ago," Dad answers before I can. "I asked for his help with marketing." He sighs. "Fine, I'll print copies so everyone can read through the contract, even though I know you won't find anything there."

***

HALF AN HOUR LATER, TO EVERYONE'S CHAGRIN, WE DISCOVER Dad was right. The contract is solid without any loopholes we could find. Emma's slouched against the couch, lost in her own head. Her dejected stance doesn't last long, though. Sitting up straighter, she turns to Dad.

"Were there any email exchanges between you and the bank?"

"Yes, several."

"And from what you remember, was the extension date ever mentioned in any of your messages?"

"Yes, a few times. But I know where your mind is going. Those exchanges aren't legally binding."

"Maybe not, but we could make a case of bad business practices on the bank's part. By failing to send you a new contract, they were negligent. A good lawyer could argue the case. It's probably a long shot that you'd win, but suing the bank will give you the extension you need."

"That's bloody brilliant," I say.

Emma's smile stretches from ear to ear, and at the same time my love for her expands. I want to breach the distance between us and kiss the hell out of her. Why did we wind up sitting on opposite ends of the room?

Dad nods once, then twice, and I can almost see the idea sinking into his head. He squares his shoulders and a little glimmer of hope returns to his eyes. He's ready for one last round before admitting defeat. "Okay, I'll call John and ask to put the process in motion."

He heads to his office, and once he's out of earshot, Keira turns to Emma. "I don't want to sound negative, but getting an extension doesn't solve the main problem. How are we going to come up with fifty thousand euros in three months?"

Emma grins like she was saving the best for last. "By turning the O'Shea Farmhouse Bed and Breakfast into the place to stay when visiting Ireland."

"That's grand, but I don't see how we'll accomplish that in so little time."

I lean forward, already knowing Emma has an ace up her sleeve. "You have a plan."

"I do have a plan. Do you remember my friend Peyton?"

When all I give Emma is a blank stare, she continues. "From the bachelorette party. She was the bride-to-be."

"Ah, well, I don't think I'd recognize her if ever saw her again. I only had eyes for one person in that group."

Emma's face turns bright pink at the same time Keira rolls

her eyes. Shit, I can't believe I said something so mushy like that. I'm definitely whipped.

"How does she fit in your plan?" I ask in a more serious tone to save face.

Emma smiles like the cat that ate the canary, then explains what she has in mind. With the efficiency of a savvy business woman, she lays it all out for us, and by the end of her impromptu presentation, I can't help thinking I'm one lucky son of a bitch.

27

EMMA

STANDING JUST ON THE OUTSIDE OF THE BIG WHITE TENT ERECTED for Keira and Clemmot's wedding reception, I take a moment to absorb everything we were able to accomplish in just a few days. My plan to transform the O'Sheas' establishment into a trendy destination all year round required we transform Keira's original low-key wedding into the stuff of dreams. The trick was doing so without blowing her original budget, but I may have contributed a little. Rori couldn't argue when I said it was my wedding gift to the couple.

To create a casual and trendy vibe, we used long picnic tables, elegant white table runners, and lush centerpieces, sticking to a crisp, neutral color palette. Romance and intimacy were achieved by the low-hanging Edison bulbs strung from a floral chandelier over the tables, giving a cool urban touch against the floral décor.

The other part of the plan, and the most important one, was convincing Peyton to attend the wedding. Like me, she's not all about parties and shopping anymore. On the contrary, she has a successful career as a lifestyle blogger with thousands of followers on social media. She's here covering the event, and tomorrow, Keira's fairy-tale wedding will be splashed all over the internet, followed by an article about the B&B. This is just the first step to bump up the reservations. The next phase of the plan is celebrity endorsement, and I'm lucky to have not one but two superstars on speed dial: Saylor, the lead singer of Wreck of the Day, and Kennedy, a rising star in Hollywood. Both my former roommates.

A local band is kicking off the party to a good start, and right now the newlywed couple is doing their thing, dancing to a mix of their favorite pop tunes and traditional Irish songs.

A light touch on my elbow makes me look to my left. Rori is standing there in a sharp suit and tie, looking yummier than ever. I get butterflies in my belly just staring at the man. His hair is pulled back in his usual bun, and his scruff has grown into a neatly trimmed beard. He's watching his sister and his new brother-in-law, but the corner of his mouth is turned upward.

"Are you enjoying the view?" he asks without looking at me.

"Yes, most definitely."

He turns with a smile and pulls me closer, gripping my hips. My arms go under his jacket and around his waist. It feels good to no longer have to use a sling. Even wearing high heels, my chin is tilted up so I can keep staring into his eyes. There's a swell of emotions swirling in my chest, threatening to burst out. I honestly don't know want to do with them. Everything is so new to me. In all the times I pictured what falling in love would feel like, my imagination never came close to the reality.

I'm smiling like a fool now because I no longer read worry in Rori's eyes, which makes me the happiest woman on earth. The last few days were hard, and I sensed that despite everyone being on board with my idea to save the business, a part of them was afraid this whole thing wouldn't work out.

"What are you thinking about?" I ask.

"I'm thinking that I'm never going to be able to thank you

enough for what you did." He touches my temple and then runs his finger down my cheek. "You don't know how much it means to me, to my entire family."

My face feels hot, and I know I must be blushing. I've never been embarrassed before by receiving a compliment, but it happens every time Rori gives me one. And I think I know why that is. He's the only person besides my father whose opinion matters to me.

"It was my pleasure to help. I'd say we did a pretty good job, huh?"

"Yes, but all credit goes to you."

I drop my gaze to the base of his throat and take a deep breath.

"It was teamwork."

Placing a finger under my chin, he brings my face back up. "You're a remarkable woman, Em. If it weren't for your guidance, we wouldn't have been able to pull it off." He pauses, his eyes turning more intense than before, as if he's searching for something in my expression. Finally, after a big intake of air, he says, "I'm about to say something that I've been putting off for a while now. But it's a truth I can't keep bottled up any longer, so please don't freak out."

Oh my God. Is Rori going to say the L-word? My heart takes off in my chest, drumming fast and hard. *Doesn't he know that asking someone not to freak out will have the exact opposite effect? If he says he loves me, can I say it back? Am I ready to say it back?*

"Emma, I—"

"There you are," Keira interrupts, and I let out the breath I was holding. I ease back from his arms and turn toward the bride.

"Hi, Keira. Are you looking for me or Rori?"

"I'm actually looking for you, Em. I have a surprise for you." Keira steps aside, revealing a figure approaching behind her. "Look who decided to crash to the party."

I gasp, covering my mouth with both hands. Declan is standing next to Keira, looking exactly how I remember him. The dark hair styled impeccably, his face clean-shaven which allows me to see his chin dimple, his suit sharp and without wrinkles. I wait for the memories of that day to assault me, to send me to a terribly dark place, but all I feel right now is overwhelming gratitude toward the man who saved my life.

Declan's blue eyes are shining, and his lips are curled into a small smile.

"Look at you," he finally says, his voice thick with emotion. "So pretty and full of life."

"All thanks to you," I reply.

"Would it be okay if I gave you a hug?"

I nod, and before I know it, I'm in his arms, crying like a baby. In all the times I thought about this reunion, I never imagined I would feel like this, finally brought back together. Undamaged.

***

Rori

I walk away, unable to stand watching Emma and Declan reunite. The way she jumped into his arms and hugged him, as if the entire world had ceased to exist, felt like a sharp knife twisting in my chest.

She was crying in his arms, for Christ's sake. *Crying*, and I know she rarely does that. My mind is going off in completely different directions, and irrationally I end up blaming my sister. Damn Keira for being so fucking helpful. I never got the chance to tell Emma how I feel, and I'm not sure if it's going to happen now. What if Emma had been right all along? What if the tragedy she shared with Declan created an unbreakable bond that no one can replace?

Before I know it, I'm at the bar, ordering a shot of whiskey, followed by a second and third. I only stop drowning my sorrows in alcohol when my father finds me.

"Where's that pretty lass of yours? I don't think I've thanked her enough for saving our place."

"She's with her hero, *Declan*." I say his name as if the guy is the scum of the earth.

"Don't tell me you're jealous, son."

I glare at Dad, who in turn watches me with amusement in his eyes. I can't remember the last time he looked at me that way, without the heaviness of regret for all that was lost.

"Of course I'm jealous. I'll never be able compete with what they have. He saved her life, for heaven's sake. He's a hero."

"In the proverbial sense, yes. But pulling a person out of the fire is not how all heroes are made." Dad's stare becomes serious before he adds, "You're my hero, Rori."

I look at him without saying a word, sure I misheard what he said, or the alcohol's already gone to my head. "What?"

He switches his attention to the dance floor, taking a sip of his drink. "I know I did you wrong, Rori. I was so caught up in the dream that I forgot you were only a kid, my son, not a project. The fact that I couldn't see how my actions pushed you over the edge kills me."

"Dad...."

He looks at me, smiling without humor. "But you pulled through. You put yourself back together without my help, and look at you now. You're a successful business owner who just might have saved my arse."

I look down at the empty glass in my hand, holding it tighter. "That was Emma's doing."

"No, it was you too. You inspire people, Rori. That's why this town cheered for your success as if it were their own. Sure, Emma had the idea, but I know without a doubt that she did it because of you. So you'd better stop with this nonsense that

Declan is better than you because he saved her. She loves you, no doubt about it. The way she watches all your moves with her heart in her eyes is proof enough. That lass is head over heels for you, lad."

I take a deep breath, hoping Dad's observations are true. Then I hug the man, something I haven't done in more than ten years. "Thanks, Da."

He hesitates for a split second before he claps my back. "Anytime, Rori. Anytime."

We break apart, and he continues. "Now, how about you go find Emma and Declan and put your mind to rest."

I nod before I go looking for them. Despite Dad's words that Emma's in love with me, I'm not going to make it easier for anyone to swoop in and take her away. I can't find Emma and Declan where I left them. Thinking maybe they headed back to the house for some privacy, I take the path up the hill with long strides, almost running.

As I'm crossing the parking lot, headlights of a car approaching make me stop. I raise my arm to protect my eyes from the glare. There's no place to park, so the car just stops in front of the house, the lights going off as the engine shuts down.

I clench my jaw when I see who's getting out of the vehicle. Alannah. It seems all the ghosts from the past decided to come out and play.

"What are you doing here?"

She keeps waking until she's right in front of me, way too fucking close, forcing me to take a step back. Her strong perfume reaches my nose, and I know if I stay in her presence for too long, the scent will give me a headache. What did she do, bathe in the stuff?

"Rori, I had to come. I couldn't let you make a mistake out of pride and stubbornness."

"Make a mistake? What are you going on about, woman? Are you drunk?"

"No, I've never been soberer in my entire life." She steps into my personal space again, touching my chest this time. "Let's put the past in the past, Rori. I hurt you and you hurt me. We were young and stupid, but I know you never stopped loving me, just like I never stopped loving you."

I must be hallucinating. That's the only explanation. Or maybe Alannah is.

I grab her wrist and push her hand off my chest. "I thought I was clear to you in Dublin. I've moved on, Alannah. I'm in love with someone else."

Her eyebrows furrow together before she shakes her head. "You haven't changed a bit. You were always so damn stubborn. But you don't have to keep pretending anymore. Simon told me what happened in Galway."

I rub my face, feeling like I'm stuck in the Twilight Zone or in one of those overdramatic soap operas Keira loves so much. Why does Simon keep butting in my business? He's like a villain who never quits.

"He told me about the fight, that you went mental when you thought I had cheated on you. I never did, Rori. Simon was lying. You have to know that."

I turn to her, staring hard, and hoping—no, *praying* I can get this through Alannah's thick head. "I don't care if you cheated on me or not. Sure, it would be fucking awful if you had done it while I was recovering in the hospital, but it wouldn't make a lick of difference in my life right now."

"I call bullshit, and I'm going to prove it." Quick as a snake, she grabs the lapels of my suit and brings my face down on hers. My entire body freezes in stunned surprise before I finally pull back.

I hear a gasp behind me, and even before I turn, I know Emma's standing there. She doesn't cry, doesn't throw angry accusations at me. She does worse—turning on her heels and running away.

"Emma, wait!" I call and take a step in her direction, only to be stopped by Alannah holding onto my sleeve.

"Let her be. It's better this way."

I pull my arm from Alannah's grasp and turn my ire on her. Holding her shoulders in a vicious grip, I yell in her face. "Get into your thick skull. We. Are. Done. I did punch Simon in his ugly mug, but it wasn't on your account." Then I let go of her, taking a step away.

The way her eyes widen and the blood drains for her face tells me I finally made it through. With trembling lips, she says, "Why would Simon lie about that?"

"Don't you get it? Simon is a psychotic son of a bitch. He lies for the sole purpose of messing with people's heads."

Alannah lets out a sob, covering her mouth. "You're the love of my life."

Her voice is nothing but a choked-up whisper. It's pitiful, and maybe I should offer her some kind of comfort, but I can't do that while Emma's thinking all sort of wrong things.

"I'm sorry, Alannah, but you aren't mine. I hope you find happiness one day."

I swing around and break into a run, not knowing where the hell Emma went.

28

EMMA

I'm not sure how long I hug Declan for, but when I ease back, Rori is no longer behind us. Keira catches me searching and is quick to say, "He wanted to give you privacy. Why don't you take a walk down the river? It'll be quieter there."

I'm torn. On one hand, I'd love to spend some time alone with Declan and finally get to know the man who didn't leave me behind. But I can only imagine what Rori must be thinking right now. I pretty much threw myself at Declan and cried in his arms. What man wouldn't be affected by that scene?

"That would be nice," Declan replies, and now I can't say no.

I give him a smile, hoping it doesn't come across as forced. Now that the emotion of seeing him again has retreated like a wave returning to the ocean, a sense of discomfort takes hold of me.

"You must think I was awful for not looking you up. I actually wanted to many times, but I wasn't sure if you wanted to see me," he says.

"I felt the same way, but in my case, I didn't think I was ready to see you."

"What made you finally change your mind?"

"My father. He had a heart attack and...." I pause because I can't tell Declan about my crazy plan. It doesn't matter now anyway. I did find what I was looking for. "Well, I felt it was about time I thanked you in person."

Declan nods and we continue down the track toward the river, which glistens quietly with the soft glow of the moon. Before we reach the river's edge, Declan stops suddenly, turning to me. "I thought about you constantly. I wondered how you were, what your life was like. It got so bad that my partner threatened to leave me."

"Wait, your partner?"

Declan nods. "I'm gay."

I open and close my mouth, but no sound comes forth.

"I know what you must be thinking, but the flirting was mutual, Emma. At the time, I didn't know what I wanted. I was attracted to women, to *you*, but I also liked the company of men. After what we went through, it put things into perspective for me. I liked women, but I knew I could only fall in love with a man. Soon after the attack, I started seeing Charlie, and the rest is history."

"That is...."

"Too much information?" He chuckles. "I'm sorry for unloading all my personal crap on you. You don't know me, and here am I blabbering about my life, but I feel like we have this special bond. Maybe it's one-sided, though."

I shake my head. "No, don't apologize. I understand exactly what you mean. I feel tethered to you in a way, but it's a pure platonic connection, so don't worry."

He lets out a loud breath and laughs. "Same on my end. I'm glad you don't think I'm a creep. And I'm sorry I missed your visit in Galway. My sister should've told me you were coming. I would've waited for you. In fact, I was crazy mad when she finally got a hold of me."

"No worries. It wasn't a wasted trip."

No, it definitely wasn't. It might've been the most important trip for Rori and me. It was then that I first realized there was no turning back from my feelings for him.

"Well, I assume since you're dating Rori O'Shea, you'll be coming this way more often? I'd love it if we kept in touch."

His comment gives me pause and he catches my hesitation. "What's wrong? Trouble in paradise?"

I shake my head. "No, nothing of the sort." Declan might be more than happy to discuss his love life with me, but I'm not ready to reciprocate. "Can I ask you a question?"

"Of course."

"Do you have nightmares, about that day?"

A dark cloud takes over Declan's eyes, and I have my answer. "Yes. Not as often anymore, though. Therapy and Charlie have been a great help in my recovery. But I still get spooked by any loud sound, and I can't be around fireworks."

"Me neither. It wasn't until recently that I was able to go underground without having a meltdown."

"Are you seeing a therapist?"

"Yes. She's helping, but I think—no, I know being with Rori has helped me more than any treatment."

"Yes, love is that powerful. I'm happy to see you thriving, Emma. I truly am."

I open my mouth to say I'm also happy for him when I hear my phone go off in my purse. I excuse myself and dig the device out. "It's my father, I have to take this." I turn slightly to answer the call. "Hello, Dad?"

"Emma, honey. I'm so glad I caught you." He sounds agitated, which is something I can't say happens a lot to him.

"What's wrong? Are you okay?"

"I'm fine. It's Patricia. She was in a car wreck, all my fault, and I'm losing my mind."

"How is she?"

"All banged up, but alive. I'm sorry to bother you, but I guess I just need to hear your voice."

"No, Dad, you did the right thing by calling me."

"I asked her to come by the house because I didn't feel like eating alone, and that's when it happened."

"She's going to be okay, Dad. Do you want me come home earlier?"

"Would you?" The hopeful tone in my father's voice does something to my chest. He sounds so terrified, just like he did when I was the one recovering in a hospital. Patricia has worked as my father's personal assistant for almost two decades. Besides me, she's Dad only constant. It's only natural for him to feel concerned, but it can't be good for his heart.

"Say no more. I'll tell Rori and we'll hop on the first flight out."

"Rori? Who's Rori? A coworker?"

Ah shit. I had forgotten that I lied to Dad about this trip being work-related.

"No, Dad. I'll explain later. Now try to relax and keep me informed. I love you."

"I love you too, honey."

I end the call and turn to Declan. "I'm sorry. I have to find Rori."

"Bad news back home?"

"Yes. My dad's assistant was in accident. She's like family to us."

"I'm so sorry. Go, don't worry about me. It was nice seeing you again, Emma."

"Likewise." I give him a quick hug, and then I'm sprinting back to the party. I go under the tent where guests are dancing or hanging by the bar. There's laughter all around us. I spot Peyton doing what she does best, her smartphone in hand capturing everything. I don't have time to explain to her that I'm leaving sooner than planned. I have to find Rori first.

But I don't see him anywhere. Maybe he went back to the house.

I hike up the long skirt of my dress and head up the rise. I hear voices in the distance—Rori is one of them, the other is a woman's. I don't think much about it until I finally reach the top and see Rori and Alannah kissing. Every part of my body freezes except for my stomach, which bottoms out through the earth. I can't draw air in, can't move a muscle. The only thing I can do is stare and die inside.

Rori pushes the woman off him and turns. The movement snaps me out of my inertia and I do what I do best—I run away. He calls my name, but there are no footsteps behind me. I'm so shocked that I can't even cry. Or maybe Declan sucked all the tears I'm capable of shedding already. Who cares? I just have to get out of here.

Since there's no pursuit, I slow down to see where I'm going. I'm near the stables, but unless I want to get to Dublin on a horse, it won't do. I swing around and retrace my steps, but instead of going around the house and back to the front, I veer toward the door that opens to the kitchen.

I find it unlocked. There are people from the catering company there, but they all ignore my presence. I continue on, not stopping until I'm back in the room I've shared with Rori for the past seven days. We've made so many wonderful memories here. I never knew what it would be like to have someone in my life who was a partner, a friend, and a great lover all packed into one. But I can't unsee that scene outside, and even though Rori pushed his ex away, he never came after me. A lonely tear escapes my eye, and I'm in the process of wiping it off when Rori comes barging into the room.

He looks at my face, then at the clothes that, without realizing it, I had begun to fold.

"Going somewhere?" he asks.

"I'm catching the first flight out tomorrow."

"So is that how this is going to be? You're not going to give me the chance to explain?"

"There's no need for an explanation. I get it. She's your first love, forever imprinted in your heart. I'll never be able to take that spot. I don't blame you for...." God, I can't even say those words.

"I know you're not stupid, so I'm going with the only other explanation. Are you mad?" He takes a step closer.

"I'm not crazy. Well, I am, a little. Who else would've come to Ireland in search of a soul mate?"

"Yes, that was a little out there, but it's not why I think you're mad. How can you think Alannah holds any piece of my heart?"

"Because she was your first." I throw my hands in the air.

"And you are my last." Rori is front of me now, his hands on my face.

"What?"

"Alannah is not imprinted anywhere in my body, much less in my heart, because you are, Emma. There's only you. You're imprinted in my heart and in my soul. I love you."

Fat and warm tears roll down my cheeks. I guess Declan didn't suck them all out of me after all. "You do?"

Rori leans his forehead against mine. "How could you not know?"

"Because I'm stupid *and* mad." I let out a shaky laugh.

"We're all a little crazy and stupid sometimes." He kisses my nose and cheeks before aiming for my mouth. I pull away.

"What's wrong?"

"Have you properly disinfected that skank off your lips?"

"What?"

Frowning, I pinch my lips and point to the bathroom. "Soap, mouthwash, toothpaste. Do whatever it takes. I'm not kissing you until every last vestige of your ex's germs are gone."

Rori shakes his head but does as I ask, disappearing into the small bathroom. This is all a ploy for me to get my act together, for me to find the courage to say those words back. Why am I so fucking nervous to say them to him? I say "I love you" all the time to my father, to my friends.

He returns a minute later and smiles at me. "I'm all clean now." He opens his arms as if he expects me to jump into them. But I don't move from my spot because I'm gathering the courage for my confession.

"Emma?" He lowers his arms, furrowing his brows. "You look like you're about to pass out." He walks around the bed and pulls me closer.

"Rori, I-I...." I bury my face in his chest as I say the words, but the sound is muffled.

"What? I got none of that."

I lift my chin and look straight into his eyes. "I said I love you!"

He flinches, and belatedly I realize that shouting the words at him wasn't the most romantic way of doing it. At first, all I feel is a slight tremor in Rori's chest right before he throws his head back and laughs from his belly up.

"That wasn't funny. It was awful," I say.

"No, lass. That was bloody funny. I can tell you've never said those words before."

I hit his chest, but he obviously feels nothing. "You know I haven't."

"I'm glad you only suck at love declarations, but you excel in other areas." He bounces his eyebrows up and down, and I don't know if I should hit him upside the head or kiss him. *Hmm, I can probably accomplish both at the same time.* He lowers his lips to mine, but when his mint-flavored tongue strokes the seam open, I can only focus on his kiss and nothing else.

After a moment, Rori says against my lips, "Now put those clothes away and let's get back to the party."

I step away, remembering why I went looking for Rori in the first place. "I have to go home."

I watch Rori's heated gaze turn into one of worry, so I quickly explain why.

He doesn't even bat an eyelash about me going home earlier, and he's absolutely adamant about coming with me, no matter how many times I tell him he should stay longer.

"Get it into your thick head, Emma. You're not getting rid of me this easily. I'm coming with you."

"Even if I have to force you to fly business class again?"

"I'll suffer through it. That's how much I love you."

29

EMMA

THE GOODBYES WERE TEARFUL, BUT THE PROMISE THAT I wouldn't let Rori go another six years without visiting Ireland made things a little easier. Peyton would stay behind and finish her assignment, but she had no doubt the O'Sheas' B&B would become the next trendy spot to stay while visiting the area.

During the flight, I couldn't help but compare it with the one that brought us to Dublin. What a difference a few days can make in someone's life.

Snuggled against Rori's chest, I ask, "Rori?"

"Hmm?"

"Are you sleeping?"

"I was. What is it, lass?

"Why did you whisper in my ear when we were about to land in Dublin?"

"No reason."

I twist my neck and look at his face. "Don't lie. You didn't like me, so why did tease me like that?"

"Who said I didn't like you?"

I lean away to properly stare at his profile. "You did?"

He smiles and caresses my face. "Emma, I began falling for

you the moment you walked into my bar and tried to sell me condoms."

"I'm not that person anymore. I want you to know that."

"What? You suddenly don't like to party anymore?"

"I do. What I'm saying is that my wild days are over."

"That's too bad. I love me some feisty woman."

I smile, knowing where he's going with that. "Don't worry, my love. You'll get that side of me any time you want."

He rubs his nose against mine, then nuzzles my neck. "Do you think we can get away with a quickie in the restroom?"

I laugh a little too loud, earning a "shhh" from the passenger across the aisle. Rori giggles with me, and I say, "Probably not."

When we land in LA, we decide to stop by the hospital to visit Patricia before heading home. In the car, I once again think about the one-eighty change in my life. It turns out I wasn't incapable of falling in love, I was just waiting for the right person to come along. It sounds crazy, but now I believe that when love is real, it happens like that, in an instant.

Playing with the button of Rori's shirt, I ask, "What happens now?"

"What do you mean?"

"I've never been in a relationship before, I don't know how to be in one."

Chuckling, he kisses the top of my head. "What makes you think I'm an expert? I've only had one serious girlfriend before."

"Funny, I always thought you dated a bunch."

"Why did you think that?"

I shrug. "Well, look at you. You're too gorgeous to stay single for long."

Rori laughs, and I'm beginning to think that sound is one my favorite things about him.

"Well, I dated, but I wasn't very lucky in that department."

"I don't want to hear the sordid details, but like I said, you should know what to do."

"Em, I was a teen when I had my first serious relationship. I had no bloody clue what I was doing. And then I dated women who thought they could control me because they were beautiful, or had money."

"Wait, wait." I raise my hand. "That's why you were so rude to me at first? You were comparing me with the others?"

Rori looks so guilty and remorseful that it's impossible to be mad at him.

"I'm sorry. And I told you I still liked you, even when all my barriers were up."

I watch him through slits before I unbuckle my seat belt and sit astride him, driver be damned. I run my long nails over his jaw, then rub my thumb over his lips. "I'm not going to hold that against you. We're human, flawed. God knows I'm terrified of you finding out about all my imperfections."

"I'm not." He runs his hand over my sternum, turning me into a pile of goo on his lap. *How can such a simple touch be so incendiary?* "You're perfect to me, even when you aren't."

"You don't need to keep saying stuff like that. I'm a sure thing."

He laughs again, spreading heat across my chest. "I'll never stop trying to woo you. And don't worry about what comes next. We'll figure it out together."

"I need to find a job." I decide to change the subject before our caresses turn into a sex show. "I can't live on my father's money forever."

"I'm sure you'll have no problem finding a job. Companies should be lining up to hire you."

"Ha, not after the stunt I pulled in New York. I also dropped my MBA, so I'm not such a hot commodity right now."

"You're too talented, Em. You're worrying over nothing."

"You're only saying that because you're my boyfriend. Shit, I have a boyfriend. My friends will never believe it. I'm still pinching myself."

"Get used to it. I'm not going anywhere. And if you want, you can always help at Closing Time. Keira thinks I should hire a manager." Rori's eyes twinkle with mirth.

"Ha-ha. I know you're not serious, but if I were the manager, the first order of business would be to get rid of that sourpuss waitress of yours."

"What? Lena?"

"If that's her name?"

"She can be a little difficult, but she's one of the best people I know. She's like a second mother to me."

"If you say so, but she'd better be nice to me next time I stop by. I am sleeping with her boss, after all." I give him a lopsided grin.

"She'll be nice because you're amazing."

"Rori, what did I tell you? I'm a sure thing."

"Excellent." He squeezes my butt.

"Don't get so excited now. There's one more thing on the to-do list to blissdom. You'll need my father's approval or this whole relationship thing is a no-go."

I didn't expect Rori to take my statement at face value, but it's amusing to watch the blood drain from his face and his eyes turn as round as saucers.

"What's your father like? Do you think he's going to mind my long hair? I can hide it under a cap. What about my job? The pub is doing well, so he doesn't have to worry that I'm going after your money, and—"

"Rori, I was kidding. My father isn't that bad. He's going to love you just like I do."

"You're only saying that because you're my girlfriend."

"Touché."

"Hey! What's that supposed to mean?"

In the end, Rori didn't have to worry about a thing. Not that there was ever any doubt in my mind that Dad would find anything wrong with the broody Irish with a soft heart. All my father cared about was that I was happy, and that was something I couldn't hide even if I tried. The little lie about my trip being work-related was forgotten. But again, Dad was distracted. He couldn't stop fussing over Patricia, asking if she needed anything. He was so over the top that even Rori noticed there's something more going on than a mere professional relationship. I guess I'd better start shopping for a bridesmaid dress.

I leave the hospital with a light heart and a pep in my step.

"Do you want me to drop you off first?" I ask.

In answer, he rubs his thumb over the inside of my wrist. "Do you want to?"

"No, but maybe you're tired."

"I'd like to come to your place, if you don't mind."

"I'd love that."

Rori

Emma no longer lives in the same apartment from when I brought her home drunk the night that feels like eons ago. Of course, I didn't expect her to, since she was still in college back then. Her new place is a cool, urban loft-style condo close to the Venice canals. It screams wealth, with newly customized details throughout and a spectacular open floor. The kitchen is the stuff of dreams with granite counter tops, a Viking stone, and a Sub-Zero refrigerator. I try my best not to feel intimidated by all this luxury. Emma is more than her money—I know that now.

The decoration is cozy, a mix of modern and reclaimed furniture, all in light colors. Extremely feminine, but not girly. I look at the large couch that could easily be dubbed as a bed, noting how perfect it is for snuggling and other things.

Emma keeps walking but I remain in place, and she stops and looks over shoulder.

"You don't want to see my room?"

"Do you really want me to?"

Frowning, she retraces her steps. "What's going on? You're acting strange."

"Do you really want me in your bed?" I move closer, forcing Emma to crane her neck to keep looking into my eyes.

"Yes, Rori. I really want you in my bed." I wasn't sure she would remember that part, but her eyes shine with understanding as her lips curl into a smile. "You know what that means, don't you?"

I throw my backpack to the side, then drop to my knees. "You were right, Emma. So here I am, on my knees, begging."

She runs her fingers through my hair before bending forward. "That was the old Emma Hart. You don't have to beg for my love, not now, not ever. It's yours, Rori. It's always been yours, even when I didn't know it."

"Good." I touch her cheek, loving the feel of her soft skin against mine. "Now come here. I'd like to try out this couch first."

With a laugh, she kisses me before we tumble to the floor, couch forgotten—at least for now.

***** THE END *****

All The Right Moves is part of Love Me, I'm Famous series universe.
Discover the other novels here.

AUTHOR'S NOTE

I sincerely hope you enjoyed Emma and Rori's love story. If you did enjoy *All The Right Moves* there are a number of ways you can help spread the word.

#1. Please tell your friends and family why they should read it. Better yet, gift it to them. If you are active on Goodreads, you can use the 'Recommend' feature.

#2. Please like the **Love Me, I'm Famous Facebook page**. When you post statuses, you can click on the smiley face button at the bottom of your post entry and select Reading, then type *All The Right Moves*. That will help your friends find purchase links and information on the novel.

#3. Please consider leaving a review for this book. It's a known fact that recommendations from friends and reviews are the most influential factors in reader's purchase decisions.

ALSO BY MICHELLE HERCULES

Paranormal Romance:

Dark Prince (Blueblood Vampires #1)

Wild Thing (Blueblood Vampires #2)

Forgotten Heir (Blueblood Vampires #3)

Reckless Times (Gifted Academy #5)

Contemporary Romance:

Wonderwall (Love Me, I'm Famous #1)

Sugar, We're Going Down (Love Me, I'm Famous #2)

Wreck of the Day (Love Me, I'm Famous #3)

Devils Don't Fly (Love Me, I'm Famous #4)

Love Me Like You Do (Love Me, I'm Famous #5)

Catch You (Love Me, I'm Famous #6)

All The Right Moves

Reverse Harem Romance:

Wicked Gods (Gifted Academy #1)

Ruthless Idols (Gifted Academy #2)

Hateful Heroes (Gifted Academy #3)

Broken Knights (Gifted Academy #4)

Lost Horizon (Oz in Space #1)

Magic Void (Oz in Space #2)

Red's Alphas (Wolves of Crimson Hollow #1)

Wolf's Calling (Wolves of Crimson Hollow #2)

Pack's Queen (Wolves of Crimson Hollow #3)

Mother of Wolves (Wolves of Crimson Hollow #4)

ABOUT THE AUTHOR

USA Today Bestselling Author Michelle Hercules always knew creative arts were her calling but not in a million years did she think she would become an author. With a background in fashion design she thought she would follow that path. But one day, out of the blue, she had an idea for a book. One page turned into ten pages, ten pages turned into a hundred, and before she knew, her first novel, The Prophecy of Arcadia, was born.

Michelle Hercules resides in The Netherlands with her husband and daughter. She is currently working on the *Blue-blood Vampires* series and the *Oz in Space* series.

Join Michelle Hercules' Reader Group:
https://www.facebook.com/groups/mhsoars

Connect with Michelle Hercules:
www.michellehercules.com
books@mhsoars.com